THE ADVE... OF
RAP KID

THE ADVENTURES OF RAP KID

MC Grammar

G

GALLERY KIDS

SIMON & SCHUSTER

London   New York   Amsterdam/Antwerp   Sydney/Melbourne   Toronto   New Delhi

MC Grammar

(aka Jacob Mitchell) is an award-winning teacher-turned-rapper and viral social-media sensation. He has won a *National Teacher of the Year* award and a *London Teacher of the Year* award, showing how engaging and exciting education can truly be!

Jacob's two passions – teaching and music – fuel his mission to make learning memorable, inclusive and (most importantly) FUN.

Recently, he headlined Young Voices nationwide arena tour with nearly 250k primary school children taking part. He was such a huge hit with parents, teachers and kids alike that they've asked him to come back again for another tour! He's been featured on Sky News, the *Daily Mail*, Capital FM, BBC News, Heart FM, BBC Radio, ITV, Channel 4, Channel 5, Made for Mums, and BAFTA, alongside the *New York Times*, *This Morning*, *BBC Breakfast* and *The Ellen Show*.

You'll recognize Jacob from *MC Grammar's Wonder Raps* and *Rap Tales* on Sky Kids and from kicking up a storm on social media, thanks to his incredible raps of popular children's books.

One of MC Grammar's proudest achievements is being the Global Ambassador for World Book Day and he has written three official songs for them.

Instagram, Facebook, TikTok, X –
@MrMCGrammar

First published in Great Britain in 2025 by Gallery Kids,
an imprint of Simon & Schuster UK Ltd

1 3 5 7 9 10 8 6 4 2

Simon & Schuster UK Ltd
1st Floor, 222 Gray's Inn Road
London
WC1X 8HB

www.simonandschuster.co.uk
www.simonandschuster.com.au
www.simonandschuster.co.in

Simon & Schuster Australia, Sydney
Simon & Schuster India, New Delhi

The authorised representative in the EEA is Simon & Schuster Netherlands BV,
Herculesplein 96, 3584 AA Utrecht, Netherlands. info@simonandschuster.nl

A CIP catalogue record for this book is available from the British Library.

ISBN 978-1-3985-3761-3
eBook ISBN 978-1-3985-3762-0
eAudio ISBN 978-1-3985-3763-7

This book is a work of fiction. Names, characters, places and incidents are either
the product of the author's imagination or are used fictitiously. Any resemblance
to actual people living or dead, events or locales is entirely coincidental.

Typeset in the UK by Sorrel Packham

Printed and bound by CPI Group (UK) Ltd, Croydon, CR0 4YY

For my G, Andrea,
and our Rap Kids:
Ellie, Khloe, Tia & Neeko

Hey, my G! Here's a secret: these chapter titles can be put together to form a **Rap Kid** rap. →

Give it a go to test out your rap skills.

Big love,
MC Grammar

CONTENTS

Mic Check, 1, 2, 3		1
1.	This Is Me!	9
2.	A Kid on a Mission With . . .	23
3.	Mr G . . . and SFX	42
4.	So, Where to Next?	59
5.	The Big Pick!	79
6.	And Then We Rest . . .	94
7.	Now It's GO TIME	95
8.	Let's Sign It!	103
9.	Plan B: We've Gotta Find It!	113
10.	Bad Rhyming or Bad Timing!	133
11.	Let's Warm Up!	142
12.	It's Time to Shine, Kid!	160
13.	We've Got This . . . We Think!	176
14.	Let's Shop for Some Bling!	190
15.	Now It's Showtime, Are You In?	205
16.	The Question Is: Will We Win?	223

MiC CHECK

1, 2, 3

Mic check, 1, 2, 3 . . . Nice to meet you, my name is Z. Virtual fist bump.

How are you, my G? (That's your new name, by the way!) You cool? Of course you are – you picked up this book, didn't you?! And IMO (in my opinion), that now makes you cooler than a polar bear in sunglasses. Anyway, welcome to the story of how I actually became Z, because **TOP SECRET**: Z isn't my real name. So this is sort of an origin story, I guess, except I don't turn into a villain at the end. NO WAY! I turn into a **RAP LEGEND** instead! No superheroes included, I'm afraid – that's a different sort of book, my G.

BUT, don't worry. This adventure is:

- ☑ BIG (as in jam-packed)
- ☑ BAD (as in good)
- ☑ LIT (as in sick) and
- ☑ LOUD! (as in pure vibes and wicked energy!)

So hold on tight and don't drop that mic (yet) because we've got A LOT to do in this book, including winning a rap battle! And yes, I said 'we'. Why? Because you're coming with me, my G, all the way.

But, before we go any further, let's set the tone with our first set of barz (a fancy street name for raps). Oh, and don't forget to join in too.

Okay, quick mic check: one two, one two! Now, DJ, drop the beat!

Wowza!

You've just found this out but,

if you take a closer look:

There's a rapper in your book!

NO WAY!

And you know who it is?

R to da A to da P to da K to da ID

It's Rap Kid!

So, yeah, that's me: Z aka Rap Kid. A young legend on a quest to become the best. Well, not just the best actually. I want to be the GOAT!*

*Sidenote 1: GOAT stands for GREATEST OF ALL TIME by the way, just in case you needed me to say. Not an actual goat. That would be weird!

Anyway, speaking of rap and rhyming, and as you can

probably tell by now: I LOVE to RHYME! Which basically makes me a rhyme-o-holic and a lyrical G (this G being short for genius). I can't help it – I was actually born this way. Rhyming is in my soul. Call it a 'gift' (or a 'curse'), or a birthmark you hear rather than see. It's like rhyming has always been part of me – bubbling in my belly and then BOOM, the lyrical lava comes rushing up and I just have to spit it out. Pure fire!

Seriously, even my first proper word, 'Mum', was quickly followed up with 'bum', which made her mad (or sad – I was too young to tell). And then when I said 'Dad' for the first time, I rhymed it with 'kebab', which made him hungry, so he went and bought a kebab and shared it with me. Result! There's a photo of baby me eating my first Greek Souvlaki! Yum!

I don't rhyme *all* the time. As I've gotten older, I've learned to control it a bit. Imagine thinking in rhyme ... That would be a nightmare. You'd never be able to think about things that don't rhyme with anything else like the words chocolate, oranges, elbows, purple – which is actually my favourite colour – and definitely not something I want to just dismiss from my life like that.

Now, I keep rhyming exclusively for when I'm writing barz in my Book of Raps, or (less exclusively) when I'm nervous and have to speak to a teacher or in front of people. That's when I DON'T have any control over it, and the rhyming gets REALLY BAD, my G! I suddenly turn into a panic pro, a quiver kid, a worry wombat . . . whatever you want to call it. Simply said: I'm a fluster of fuss when it comes to pressure and public speaking. Do you know what I mean? Class presentation? No thanks! Speaking in front of the whole school in assembly? Just not for me, my G. I know *They* say practice makes perfect when it comes to public speaking, but for me it just seems to make trouble.

Quick disclaimer: If I get nervous at any point during this epic adventure and start excessively rhyming, don't worry, I just need to go through my two-step-system motions:

1. I'll make fresh cup of anxieTEA (best served hot).
2. I will rhyme and rhyme . . . and RHYME my way out of, or into even more, trouble!

But, here's where you come in to save me. If any of the above does happen or we do encounter a public speaking pressure scenario, just shout:

HE'S A RAPPER! GET HIM OUTTA HERE!

Thanks, bro!*

*Sidenote 2: You'll notice that I say `bro' a lot. This doesn't mean I think we're related in any way. It also has nothing to do with gender. It's just my way of saying mate, homie, pal, BRF (Best Rapper Friend), or BRFF (Best Rapper Friend Forever). It basically means we're so close and so cool that we could be family.

Get it, BROmeo? Sorry, I can't help it! I can just tell you're a cool cat**, and I am so excited to have you come on this adventure with me.

**Sidenote 2.5: I don't actually think you're a cat. It's just a saying from the olden days that means you're all right. You know: as in you're cool, laid-back, easygoing.

Anyway, that's enough for the intro. It's time to turn the page so you can join me on this next-level adventure to go from a quiet, classroom kid to a straight-up RAP LEGEND (who hopefully goes on to win the greatest rap competition in the world and then becomes the GOAT). Pretty straightforward plan really. You ready to roll? Fist bump if you're in:

That's that sorted then. Great to have you on board, my G. Now let's goooooooooooooooo!!!*

Sidenote 3: I almost forgot . . . if some of the words I say in this book don't make sense to you, it's probably because you ain't a G from the underground rap scene like me . . . yet! But don't worry, BROseph, I've got your back. How? Well, I've taken the liberty of putting together a rap dictionary/glossary thingamajig at the back of the book for you to use whenever you need a translation or vocab breakdown. See, I told you I've got your back. Thank me later!

No, seriously, do thank me, 'cause putting it together took aaaaaggggeeeeeesssss!

Speaking of time . . . it's SHOWTIME! See you in chapter one, BROski!

CHAPTER 1

This Is Me!

NEWS FLASH! NEWS FLASH! THIS JUST IN:

Rap Kid wins! A number-one album, the biggest-selling song of the year, a killer clothing line and now he's officially the Golden Mic Royal Rap Rumble: Battle of the Barz champion! Can anyone or anything stop this young legend from dominating the rap world?

Nope! Absolutely NOT! I told ya, this is meant to be, my G. The fire barz, the fresh garms, the sick cars and my

name in bright lights: I'm a rap superstar! It's in my baggy genes! LOL. Get it? In fact, with all of this success (and this drip, of course), sources say you can see me shining from the moon. And that's the truth, Ruth!*

*Sidenote 4: Wait, just to be clear, I'm not saying your name is Ruth by the way, unless it actually is which is pretty sick – hi, Ruth! 'Ruth' just happens to rhyme with 'truth', so that's why I said it.

See, I told ya, I can't help myself: always rhyming and always shining! And climbing and designing and redefining . . .

STOP!

(See, that was the point when you were meant to shout out: HE'S A RAPPER! GET HIM OUTTA HERE! Next time, my G, next time!)

'Wake up, you daydreaming wasteman!'

Oops! Was I daydreaming again?

Uh-oh. I know that voice, and that smell: the combination of Badboy 2.0 aftershave and hot HATERade breath can only mean one thing. It's Bully Boy! Yep, that's his name and his game. The biggest bully in town and he's always in my face and space like a mosquito on Dracula's burrito. A proper pest!

'Fantasizing about being a famous rapper again, loser? Ha! As if.'

He knows I won't answer, just in case I rhyme and say

something silly in front of everyone, so I stay quiet. As usual. That's why they call me Z after all. Z means zero. Zero words. Zilch! And while I am not a fan of it as a name, I know there's just no point in me saying something. Why? If I do, it will rhyme and they'll all laugh at me. And that's even worse!

'Thought so! Well it's time to wake up, big man, 'cause you actually need a voice to be a rapper. Your barz are weak and your flow is dead.'

Bully Boy's posse are pointing at me. Here we go AGAIN. I like to call them The Snicker Squad or The Ha-Ha Hooligans 'cause of the way they chuckle and giggle to their phony homies. So predictable.

WAIT! Bully Boy's got my Book of Raps!

A billion words are bubbling inside my mind right now like the word 'no', but . . . I'll probably rhyme that with 'bro' and he's defo not my bro!

Or the word 'wait', but then I might rhyme that with 'mate' and that's something we'll never be, so I'm staying quiet just to be sure.

Oh no! He's not going to do what I think he is with my book, is he? (Instead of OMG, I say OMD – it means 'oh my days'.)

OMD! He is. I can't even grab it from his hands because they're way too high in the sky for me to reach.

Too late. He's done it. He's thrown my Book of Raps across the class like a frisbee. And guess what? It's hit Mrs Malinki on her head. Uh-oh!

THIS.

IS.

NOT.

GOOD.

I mean, she already hates me after my first day in her class when I accidentally said, 'Yes, Mrs Malinki', and then I rhymed it with 'stinky' when she called my name for the register. I told you, I can't help it! So now I just nod or raise my hand, but she's never forgotten. Neither have I.

And now I'm definitely in for it! See, this rhyming can be a dangerous game, my G, so that's exactly why I stay quiet most of the time and just write all of my thoughts down on paper instead. It's a lot safer, trust me!

It's also a great way to get things off your mind. Here, check out this rap I wrote about Bully Boy. If you like it, you can try rapping it too. Let's GO!

A Rap About Bully Boy

Once upon a time in a faraway land,

Bully Boy lived with his Bully Boy gang.

One day he went for a walk and fell

Into the oblivion.

Oh well!

Ha! That was jokes! As you can tell, I am not a Bully Boy fan. Or a fan of bullies in general. The words 'my life' and 'nightmare' have come together in helly-matrimony since he face-planted into my world.

ARRRGGGGGGGGHHHH!

Sorry, I had to let that out. You know that feeling you get when you just wanna scream really loudly to get some of that frustration out? Happens to the best of us. And, here are some simple steps if you really want to nail it:

1. Look up at the sky. A variety of backdrops can work for this: green field, urban jungle, bedroom window.

2. Clench both of your fists till your knuckles turn pale or throb a little.

3. Drop to your knees. The more dramatic the better. Puddles are even more theatrical if there's one nearby (but not essential).

4. Scream the word 'argh' really loudly whilst shaking your fists in the air, still looking up at the sky.

How did you get on? Trust me, it is a great way to feel better. And it looks really impressive!*

Sidenote 5: You've probably realized by now that I'm a bit rampant when it comes to a tangent! My mind just bounces from one thing to another. I call it a brain wave. I'll be thinking and talking about one thing and then SPLASH! Another thought comes crashing down and takes over! So stay alert, my G, 'cause this adventure is going to have a ton of brain waves. In other words, there will be lots of side stories in the big main story . . . if that makes sense? It's just how I roll, sorry. (Not sorry!)

Anyway, snap-back to reality and Mrs Malinki is vexed and stomping towards me like a hungry raptor. And nah, not the cute one, Blue, from that movie. This dinoROAR can't be tamed. She is absolutely fuming! There's actual smoke blowing from her ears like she just drank a smoothie mix of extra hot sauce, a Sichuan hot pot AND a vindaloo. Extra spicy!

'What do you have to say for yourself, young man?'

Silence. Cue the tumbleweed and Wild West music.

'Silence. Again. Fine! Off you go to Mr Grimewood's room.'

Now, I know what you're thinking: the 'Grime' in his name must come from the street word 'grime' as in grime music, the genre you emcee over or rave to, right? And with that logic, Mr Grimewood must be some kind of famous street DJ, correct? Well, sorry to break it to you like Father Christmas's foot through a gingerbread house, but this ain't that kinda party, BRObama. Nope! Grime (in our school) is more likely to come from the dictionary definition:

Grime

/grʌɪm/ A layer of dirt on the skin or a building

Synonyms: filth, muck, gunge . . .

I couldn't have put it better myself, 'cause our 'Grime' is all of the above, except he gets UNDER our skin and is

ALL OVER the school building. EVERYWHERE! You should see the state of his office – proper grotty. Let me break it down for you in detail: he has a bald head like a boiled egg, a hungry caterpillar monobrow, a total of eight teeth and the smallest ears you've ever seen. Imagine two walnuts on the side of your head and you've sorta got the picture.

There's even a rumour going around that Mr Grimewood is actually heartless. As in he has no heart! Far-fetched, I know, but apparently they weren't giving out hearts the day he was born, years and years and years ago, which means he now just has an angry dance DJ in the middle of his chest blaring a booming bassline to pump blood around his big, burly body. The guy is proper strict and I'm now heading straight to his room of doom.

DUM!
DUM!
DUM!

A few minutes later

(Tip for the future: stalling for a
little while adds dramatic effect.)

Knock knock!

'Come in!'

He's screaming already. Wowza! This doesn't look good, my G. Whatevs, I'm going in . . . And BOOM! There it is: over the massive desk is his bald, shiny head – and it looks like this egg is ready to crack!

'What did you do this time, Z?'

He ain't even looking up from his pile of important teacher stuff. He's probably reading some old-skool manual about how to be the meanest headteacher on the planet. I suppose everyone's gotta have dreams about being good at something, don't they?

You know the deal by now, my G: I'm not responding because if I do, I just KNOW I'll say the wrong thing. Like call him 'SLIME' instead of 'GRIME', or 'egg preacher' instead of 'headteacher'.

'Z, if you don't answer me, I will assume you did in fact throw your silly little book of words at Mrs Malinki . . .'

Nope! Still not replying.

He's looking at me, and now another crack has appeared on his egg head. I'm not YOLKing! Get it? LOL! Woah! Okay, when I say 'crack', I mean 'vein'. Big and bogey-green. So big it's like a beanstalk about to sprout – bigger than the one Jack climbed to grab that golden hen. But there's no golden hen here, just a giant – and it looks like he's ready to blow!

Again, I ain't saying a thing. There's no way I'm going to chance a rhyme with Grime. N to the O! I feel like there's steam coming off his head and it's making the room smell like eggs, so it's time to get out of here before I end up fried, poached or scrambled!

'Fine! You want to play it the hard way. Then it's two weeks of detention before and after school starting Monday. Now, get out. Your face is offending my *feng shui*!'

Holy Quackamole! I did not EGGspect that. That's a low blow! But hey, at least I can leave the room of doom and go and find my Book of Raps back in class. Yep, that's the mission, and you're coming with me, BRObi-Wan Kenobi, so let's roll on to chapter two!

It's time for MISSION BOOK GRAB. LET'SSSSSS GOOOOOOOOO!

CHAPTER 2

A Kid on a Mission With . . .

There it is! I can see the book, my G. Winner, winner, chicken dinner! Woah, but wait! Mrs Malinki is sitting next to it. What? She usually goes to the staff room for lunch. Oh man, my mission is over before it's even started!

Waaaaaaaaaaaaaaaaaaaaaaaaaaaaa!

(FYI: that was one of those baby cries you see toddlers doing lying on the floor in the middle of a supermarket. You know? The ones where their mouths are open wide, and you can see they're so upset but no sound is coming out, until . . .)

((((GONG!))))

Woah! What was that?

'Stop crying, young padawan!'

Huh? That wasn't the toddler tantrum sound I was expecting. In fact, who is that?

⟨⟨⟨⟨ GONG! ⟩⟩⟩⟩

'Rappers never quit, Z. You must be at one with the problem and only then will you reach the true solution.'

Ah! I know who that is now! It's my inner **WARRIOR**. Should have known from the GONG sound. Trust me when I say that things are about to get pretty DEEP, my G. Yep, whenever you hear that sound, it'll be him. Unless the GONG is a little more high-pitched, then it's likely to be my inner *WORRIER*. They both have a habit of

popping up with their thoughts in times of desperation or decision-making.

I like to think of them as my INNER CHICKEN vs INNER CHAMP. They don't always agree, which means I am often left feeling proper confused and bamboozled! Here's what's happening right now in my head:

WARRIOR vs *WORRIER*

WARRIOR: You can do it, Z. I believe in you.

WORRIER: Don't you dare, kid! If you get caught, it's all over.

WARRIOR: Fear is a reaction. Courage is a decision. Make the right one, my son.

WORRIER: Actually, fear is an indicator, like in a car, and you should do a U-turn and get away pronto!

WARRIOR: It's never wrong to fight for what is right!

WORRIER: *There will be no fighting in school and certainly no stealing that book back!*

See! It's so annoying. I mean, what would you do if you were me right now, my G?

You know what? Let's have some fun! Why don't you let me know what you would do by ticking below:

☐ Do the BIG-MAN-TING and go for it. Full 100!
☐ Act like a lost chicken who just bopped into a fried chicken shop by mistake and GET OUT OF THERE ASAP!*

*Sidenote 6: Hey, can I just say that I know that we've just sorta met, but I'm getting the vibe that you'd go for it, so I will too. I have to!

There are so many sick lyrics and proper bangers in that book from back in the day (infants) right up to this very moment (almost secondary school), I can't just let it go to the Paper Recycling Gods, Lost Property Lord or, worst case, the King and Queen of Confiscation. If that happens, the world may never get to hear my classic raps . . . like 'The Chicken Fajita Rap'.

Check this out:

The Chicken Fajita Rap

This is a rap about wraps.

I'm a rapper and a wrapper, how's that?

I've got a red onion and a pepper

in my hand,

And sizzling chicken in a pan.

Ooooh, or the one I wrote about the smelliest fart in Europe that goes like this:

The Smelliest Fart in Europe

Everybody get out,

Everybody run!

I can feel something humming in my bum.

Everybody escape,

Everybody flee,

I can feel it coming on the count of three!

1 . . .

2 . . .

3 . . .

(Insert your best fart sound here)

Now, fire away! Literally, LOL!

Anyway, as I told ya: there are some absolute stonkers (and some absolutely bonkers ones) in there, so there's no way I'm letting Mrs Malinki take them! Bet she wants the raps for herself to hijack my future superstardom. Yeah, that's it! Well, I'm saying NO to the WAY and we're going in, fam! Decision made.

But first, we need an action plan.

And do you know what *They* say the best plan of action is? DISTRACTION!

Actually, while we're on the subject of *They*, who actually are *They* with all of this advice and bla, bla, bla quotes? Seriously, who does say all of this stuff? People – mums, dads, teachers, in particular – always say, 'Well, you know what *They* say . . .' and then reel off some wise piece of advice that's centuries old. Doesn't make sense! We listen to *them* all the time, but we don't even know who *They* are! I mean, *They* might not even be that wise.

Warning: It's time for a brain wave!

Just for fun, I have put together some of *They*'s greatest hits below, alongside some of my totally-more-than-acceptable responses:

- **THEY** say never meet your heroes. Ridiculous! I've met my local ice-cream-van owners, a power couple called Milly and Vanilli (bet he invented the flavour vanilla), and they're absolute LEGENDS in the ice-cream-van community. Let me tell you, I've met them many times and they've always hooked me up with an extra flake, or drizzle of strawberry sauce. So IMHO (in my HUMBLE opinion) they're still massive heroes of mine.

- **THEY** say Rome wasn't built in a day. Durrrr! This is obvious, isn't it? The temporary traffic lights in my endz have been there for three weeks now and the council are just fixing a burst water pipe! So how would you build a whole city in a day? Nonsense!

- **THEY** say love makes the world go round. Hmmmmm. I'm pretty sure the cause of the Earth spinning on its axis is actually gravity and its

relationship with the sun. Pretty obvious then that the *They* who said this, must have failed science at school.

○ **THEY say that the pen is mightier than the sword.** Yeah, maybe in a poetry slam or rap battle, but I am pretty sure that no matter how hard your barz and raps are, you ain't winning a sword fight against a knight with just your pen, my G!

And finally: saving the best (or most deluded) till last . . .

○ **THEY say the early bird catches the worm.** Right, and what about the innocent little worm, aye? What about if he/she/they were to listen to this little nugget of advice too? Then what happens? Picture it: the little worm waking up at the crack of dawn checking his Instagrub, only to see such profound advice from *They*. Then, feeling motivated

and inspired, they (the worm) head out confidently before anyone else in Worm World with their coffee and croissant ready to seize the day. Oh, but look who else is up early and has just seen the same wise post: the EARLY BIRD. Now what?

Disclaimer: Skip this next part if you're squeamish or if you have a pet worm.

Shall I tell ya? Ready? DEATH! Gory, gruesome, horrible DEATH! Why? Because of *They*. *They* said, 'the early bird catches the worm!' and the early bird did! It caught it and it KILLED it! 'Cause birds like to eat worms! So, with that in mind, and this goes out mainly to all of the worms out there: STAY IN BED, little worm! BE LATE, little worm! BE LAZY, little worm and you'll be ALL GOOD! Oh, and don't ever listen to *They* and their terrible advice again!

Anyway, now I've got that off my chest. It's GO TIME. Thankfully, I do some of my best strategic thinking when the rest of my brain is off on a tangent. So, my G, this is how I am gonna get my Book of Raps back (cue evil laugh).

Check this out:

STAGE 1

Step 1: Open the classroom door, just a crack. This requires precision – open it too far and it will creak and alert Mrs Malinki to my presence.

Step 2: Shimmy and shuffle my butt into the crack. A crack in a crack! Get it? LOL LOL LOL LOL and LOL!

Step 3: Pull my own pinky finger and . . .

Step 4: Drop the BASS! (That's the fart, by the way.)

Step 5: Let it linger. Mmmmmmmm.

Step 6: Waft. (This is when you use your hands like a fart fan to spread the love.)

As soon as Mrs Malinki feels the true wrath of this stinky dinky and goes to open the window, it's time for stage two of the plan.

STAGE 2

Step 1: (Well, it's sorta step seven, but you know what I mean): Breathe in!

Step 2/8: Hold nose.

Step 3/9: Stay low. Smoke rises, remember?

Step 4/10: Using only two pinky fingers, do a power-push up to rise high like Bruce Lee and then grab the book!

Step 5/11: Ninja roll out of there and breathe. Wooooooosssssaaaaaaa!

Okay, you ready to go, my G? Good, me too!

I'm going in!

Creeeeeaakkkkkkkk!

Shhhhhhh!

Shimmy.

Slowly . . . slowly.

The butt has arrived, a first-class delivery. Amazon Prime time!

Right, we're in position, so the only thing left to do: vaporize! Repeat after me.

Eyes closed.

Cheeks squeezed.

Deep breath in.

Pinky finger up.

Now, just one pull of this finger and there's no turning

back . . .

3 . . .

2 . . .

1 . . .

'Stop!'

Wait, that's Mr G's voice. Oh, allow it, man! I was so

close . . .

'What are you doing, Z?'

I'm saying nothing. Now he's just looking at me,

surveying the scene like he's ready to call the Grime-scene investigator, aka Mr Grimewood, to analyze the evidence. Eleven-seventeenths of my eyes are closed, hoping that if I can't see him, he can't see me. The only problem is 110% of my butt is still deep in the classroom.

'Z, is there a reason why your bum is stuck in a classroom door?'

Again, silence. I'm saying nada, nowt, zilch, diddly squat!

'Whatever you're doing, Z, I want you to stop and come with me. There's someone I want you to meet.'

Meet?

Who?

But I've still got stages four to eleven of my masterplan to execute, remember? Oh, whatevz! Let's GO! I want to see who this mystery person is, and I actually like Mr G. He's cool. Not a *cool cat*, but cool for a teacher. Definitely 'my G' potential, if he wasn't a teacher. He dresses smart – not street smart, but smart for a teacher. Always a shirt and tie at least. Sometimes a jacket as well. Do you have a cool teacher in your school, my G?

'Oh, and hurry up if you want this book back!'

OMD! My Book of Raps is in Mr G's hand. NO WAY!

Coming! I say in my head, of course, as I'm running to catch up with him. I'm keeping my eyes on the ground just in case looking at him reminds him to interrogate me about why my bum was stuck in Mrs Malinki's classroom door. Looking at the ground ain't a bad thing, especially if you get to spot a sick pair of kicks, and Mr G always wears wicked ones with his suits. That's how I know he has the potential to be a G, not just a *Mr* G. That's a golden rule in my book: you can always tell by someone's choice in footwear their level of cool.

Warning: It's time for a brain wave! In fact, here's my official guide to selecting the right footwear, just in case.

CREP CHECK

1. Keep it simple. Keep it classic.

2. Never exceed the two-flourish rule. Whether its colourful laces, light-up soles or a neon heel, LESS IS MORE. Going too hard means you're trying too hard.

3. Laces can either be purposefully untied or tucked in. NEVER neatly tied in a bow. That's ordinary. And ordinary can never be EXTRAordinary.

Sorry about that. Another sneaky brain wave. But now we're back and at least I have my Book of Raps (well, sorta), and I'm off to meet a mystery guest. It could be worse. Like what's going on with my guts right now. FYI: I actually really do need to fart. Maybe I prepped too hard. And I've heard that if you hold a fart in it can end up leaking out of your mouth when you speak. Nah, my G, I ain't letting that happen! This twisting tornado is coming out now from its rightful exit point, so hold on tight!

3 . . .

2 . . .

1 . . .

BRRRAAAAAAAAPPPPPPPPP!!!!*

*Sidenote 7: That's the sound a roadman makes when he
farts, by the way! True story!

Ooooo wee! That's the last time I am having a Mungo's Chicken meal-deal special offer — I knew those one-star DripAdvisor reviews must have meant something.

I'll tell you what, why don't you move on to the next chapter. I'm just gonna hang here for a second just in case there's any unfinished business . . . you know: a second wind, literally. I'll see you in a second, BROprah.

Oh, and thanks for hangin' with me.

Fist Bump!

CHAPTER 3

Mr G . . . and SFX

Right. We're here: Mr G's room. The sickest room in the school, decked out wall-to-wall with amazing instruments, whizzy computers, big booming speakers, golden microphones and those DJ mixer things with all of the gizmos and gadgets. Oh! And that super-cool spongey soundproof stuff – you know like what you see in all of the rap videos and big Hollywood music studios. Love this place! It's so cool and so creative, just like Mr G. Within the cool parameters legally allowed for teachers of course!

They say that when Mr G first started working here, Grime didn't want to let him deck out the décor and finesse the place with his music equipment. But then Mr G explained that he uses it for teaching lessons, and everyone started getting better grades, so Grime had no choice but to let him keep it all. That's how the legend goes anyway . . . Speaking of legend, who is Mr G standing next to . . . ?

Hmmmmm. Not seen this kid before. Must be a newby – you know, a rookie. Cool look though: fresh high-top creps, baggy jeans, white tee, snapback and a slick denim jacket peppered with awesome, uber-colourful graffiti, with each tag spelling out a cool quote like: 'Live your best life', 'Too blessed to be stressed' and 'It's cool to be kind'. Maybe I forgot to mention but my school doesn't have a uniform policy, which is probably the only cool rule this place has. The rest of the rules are proper old-skool. I'm talking like back in the day of Miss-Trunchball-forward-slash-Queen-Victoria. That sort of vibe. Not old-skool as in retro tuuuuuuuuuuunes and vintage clothes!

To give you a better sense of what I mean, here's three of the rules. Three of the worst, in my opinion. And yes, you know the deal by now: I have also taken the liberty of including my completely reasonable responses:

1. **No seasoning!** And no I'm not talking about the spring, summer, autumn, winter seasons. We all know that being a meteorologist requires little to no accuracy anyway. What I'm talking about is the flavour (or lack of) of the school canteen food! I'm pretty sure, the word 'flavour' is actually a word these chefs ain't even heard of, trust me! The same goes for the words palatable, yummy, scrumptious, tender, tasty . . . As a matter of fact, when it comes to food these lot are connoisseurs in the bland, dry, plain and straight-up BORING! That's why there's always a little backup bottle of hot sauce in my backpack. SNM!

2. **Snacks brought in from outside of school can't have a packet or be made in a factory and must therefore be grown naturally!** Rewind, selector!

Say that again . . . That's what you're thinking, right? Yep, me too! And to put it plain and simple: crisps, chocolate, sweets and cakes are all cancelled in my school! Not even on fish-and-chip Friday. Terrible behaviour!

3. **To use the toilet in lesson time, you need a toilet pass.** And, if you are caught without one, you receive a week's detention before AND after school. Oh, and only one person can go at a time from each class. One second: what if I'm desperate? What if I am bursting like a balloon, better yet a hot-air balloon, actually, a WATER BALLOON? (Except it ain't filled with water, if you get what I'm saying?) And then when I go to ask, someone has already just gone from my class? What then, aye? It won't be pretty, will it?

Anyway, that's enough of that. Back to reality . . . and the new kid on the block: the mysterious girl.

Woah! I think she just looked at me. Shall I smile at her?

100% ☐   No, that's corny, bro! ☐

Too late! My smile never fails.

But wait, this time it has.

She didn't even flinch. Nuda. I know: another smile will do it. She must have missed the first one. This time it's gonna be one of those weird ones where you scrunch your nose, squeeze your cheeks and then your neck juts forwards followed by a little nod. The type of smile you do to strangers to be polite when your mum wants you to say hello to them. You know the kind I am talking about. Shall I do it?

Yep! ☐   Allow it! ☐

I'm going for it, my G . . .

Again, nothing. Okay, one last try, but this time with words. After all, I am a legend when it comes to words, so

46

I can't fail here. Well, I can, but I'm hoping I won't, because even though I've just met this kid and she hasn't spoken or smiled yet, I kinda like her. And to keep things short, sweet and straight to the point, I'm going for the classic and charismatic welcome greeting.

'You cool, fam?'

What! Not even an inch of a flinch of acknowledgement. And now her head is bowed fully down so all I can see is the top of her hijab. Bare rude! It's a cool hijab though.

'Z, this is Essef.'

Oh yeah, I forgot Mr G was here too.

'Essef?' I roll the name around my brain. It's different, but it suits her.

'Yes, Essef Xubair, or Essef X,' Mr G replies.

'Essef X as in SFX?' I ask.

Mr G nods.

'Short for sound effects?'

He nods again.

Cool name. And I nod too because it's cool to nod at

cool things. I wonder if she's a sound effects specialist.

'SFX has just started here, Z,' Mr G says before I can ask. And before you ask – I know I've spent pages and pages explaining that my name is Z because I never talk at school, but it's different with Mr G. I trust him and he gets me, so I can be me, if that makes sense? Glad we got that sorted! Anyway, he's about to say something else.

'I've been keen for the two of you to meet. I think you'd make an awesome dynamic duo.'

Duo? I don't ask it out loud, but my face must show my question because Mr G answers.

'Yes, I can see it now: Z and SFX! You spit barz, and SFX drops beats,' he declares.

It's bait, but I can't help but look at her for her response. She ain't saying a wor—

Huh! Did someone just say 'boots'?

'CATS!'

Wait? And who just said 'cats'?

'BOOTS AND CATS AND BOOTS AND CATS AND BOOTS AND CATS AND BOOTS!'

It's SFX! She's beatboxing, and she's sick!

'BOOTS AND CATS AND BOOTS AND CATS AND BOOTS AND CATS AND BOOTS . . !'

Just copy what she's doing and you can beatbox too, my G! Seriously, my eyes are popping and my head is bopping right now! She's a legend at this! OMD!

'I knew you'd be gassed, Z. SFX is a beatboxer and uses sound effects to express herself. She doesn't like to speak much either. Isn't that right, Essef?' Mr G asks.

SFX points at her jacket.

'Come a little closer, Z,' Mr G encourages.

I step forwards and squint at what she's pointing to on her jacket. I see it. NO WAY! Those aren't just random quotes on her jacket – they're responses. You know, the answers to questions people might ask her. And right now, she's pointing to the words 'True Story'.

Mind blown!

'So let me get this straight. She literally spits beats and I write rhymes?'

'Yep! A match made in heaven, especially when there's something super special coming to town next month.' Mr G chuckles as he walks towards his massive classroom cupboard and disappears into it.

Talk about a mysterious exit. Seriously, he's proper left us hanging in here . . .

Actually, scrap that. He's back! I was just being impatient.

'Aha! Here it is! Have a look at this.' He walks towards us with a flyer in his hand but I can't see what it says.

And for the first time, SFX takes a step forwards and looks at me. She's either warming up to me or she just really wants to see what's on the flyer too.

AMATEUR RAPPERS WANTED

THE ROYAL RAP RUMBLE:

BATTLE OF THE BARZ

IS COMING TO TOWN

CASH PRIZE

FOR THE WINNER AND

THE ILLUSTRIOUS WORLD-FAMOUS

GOLDEN MIC TROPHY

DO YOU HAVE WHAT IT TAKES?

NO WAY! A real-life rap battle. Just like in the movies. And they want amateur rappers to sign up! What do you think, my G? Do I have what it takes?

'So I think you two should enter,' Mr G says as he hands us a pen to fill out the application form.

'Us?!' SFX and I ask at the same time, which makes Mr G chuckle again.

'Uh-huh, and I am going to be your coach.'

'Us?!' we ask again.

'Yep! You two!'

'But, Mr G, you're not thinking this through. How am I going to get on stage and spit barz in front of hundreds of people when I haven't even rapped in front of my own mum before?'

'You're going to work together as a team. You won't have to get up alone – SFX will be with you. And I have already thought of your name,' he says, clearly buzzing with himself.

We both look at him expectantly.

'Beatz 'n' Barz! You've got the barz —' he points to me — 'and you've got the beatz —' he points to SFX.

We look at each other again, and I can see she's feeling just as nervous about all this as me. Maybe even more nervous. I mean, she started a new school today as well. That's a lot for one person to process. New school, teachers, people — and now thrust into the spotlight for the performance of a lifetime. No pressure. This must be how contestants feel on those reality shows . . . Except they sign themselves up for those, so not the same AT ALL.

Beatz 'n' Barz. I do like it though. It's got a bit of a ring to it.

'Beatz and—'

'Barz,' SFX finishes. And she smiles too, which cements the friendship and seals the deal. Partners in crime! Or should I say 'rhyme'? LOL!

'You like it?' I ask her.

She points to another phrase on her jacket. 'HELL TO THE YEAH!'

RiiiiiiiiNNNNNGGGGGGGGGGG!

Oh no, that's the school bell. Lunchtime's over! What a buzzkiller!

'One more lesson until the weekend, you two. On Monday, Beatz 'n' Barz boot camp begins! Now hurry up or you'll both be late. Remember, every moment counts!'

In another life, Mr G could definitely have been a motivational speaker because I am feeling proper gassed right now and like we can definitely win the Royal Rap Rumble.

Wait: Brain wave! What makes it royal? Do you think the King will be there, my G? Now that would epic, but at the same time I think I'd be shaking like a leaf in a hurricane!

RiiiiiiiiNNNNNNGGGGGGGGGG!

Second bell! I really have gotta go. We'll have to sign up for the competition later! See you on the flipside**, my G. Thanks again for rollin' with me still; I guess you're part of the crew now. In fact, let's make it official!

Beatz 'n' Barz and _____

(insert your name here). Hopefully it's a sick rapper name*!

*Sidenote 8: If you can't think of a sick rapper name, you can use my name `rap name´ generator at the back of the book. See, as I said before, I've always got your back, my G!

**Oh, and when I said flipside a second ago, I meant in the next chapter. Don't go trying a crazy backflip or anything. I'm not insured for injuries or damage.

Peace out, BRO-yo!

CHAPTER 4

So, Where to Next?

Why do they have a 'last lesson' on a Friday anyway? Everyone knows that every kid in the world uses this lesson to think about their weekend and all of the *evil*— Whoops! I mean *awesome* plans they have. And that's exactly what I'm doing. And I bet that's what you do as well, am I right, my G?

My S-Days Strategy is simple ('S-Days' is Saturday and Sunday, by the way):

- Write barz
- Spit barz

- Eat chocolate barz to help inspire me to write EVEN MORE barz

I'm a Sp-BAR-tan! Get it? Ha ha!

Anyway, in approximately four minutes, seventeen seconds and forty-two milliseconds I am out of here and the Royal Rap Rumble preparations officially begin. And, in the time I've just said that it's now only four minutes, eight seconds and eleven milliseconds till I can yell at the top of my lungs, 'Adios! Au revoir! Antío! Sayonara! And erm . . .' Wait, I swear I know another cool way of saying goodbye. Hmmmmm . . . what is it again? That's it! 'LATERZ!'

Riiiiiiiinnnnnngggggggggggggggg!!!

And there it is: the bell has rung. Gassed! School is done, it's Fri-yay! and I am going home to prepare for superstardom. Wait? Should I go and say goodbye to SFX?

Nice thought, but to be honest I'm about three smiles ahead already and I don't wanna come across as too keen. So let's go HOME!

First stop: the bus stop. Doh! (said in the Homer Simpson voice.) Look at the queue; that is bare long! Might not even make it onto the first bus at this rate, and that's never a good thing! Why? Everyone knows that if you miss the first bus, you end up on the second bus. And who's always on the second bus? The Famous Five aka The Late Kids aka The Secondary School Lot!

FYI: The Famous Five are made up of five core groups. Allow me to break it down for you in universal school language. I promise, whatever school, town, city or country you're from, you're gonna know exactly who I'm talking about:

Group 1: The Bullies. Yep, that includes your royal slyness, Bully Boy. They're BIG. They're BAD! And they just wanna be loved, IMO.

Group 2: The Populars. You know, the famous faces in school that everyone adores and wants to be like. Picture perfect, like they've always got a Snapchat filter on their face. Oh, and this is the group where you'll definitely find the Prom Queen and King, captains of the sports teams and, of course, the cheerleaders. So High School Musical . . . bore off!

Group 3: The Goths. Love their style, but OH MY DAYS it's hard to stand up and hold on to the yellow bus strap thingmajig or pole when you're sandwiched between a mohican and a spiky-studded leather necklace. Ouch!

Group 4: The Lads. You know the type. 'Here we go, here we go, here we go!' and 'You're not singing any more!' except they are singing. They naturally migrate through school in packs, and spit for fun. Butters!

And finally, **Group 5: The Drama Kings and Queens.** Don't get me wrong, I love music, singing and dancing, but these guys ARE THE DRAMA. The last thing anyone wants to hear on a Friday afternoon is a choral rendition of 'Defying Gravity' that isn't anywhere close to being as good as the original. That ain't 'WICKED', and by that I don't mean 'wicked' as in good like that tune that goes 'wicked, wicked, junglist massive'. Nope! I mean it as in bad 'wicked' like a green-skinned wicked witch of the West End, or what the dictionary definition says 'wicked' is, which I have taken the liberty of including below for you. It'll keep your parents happy if they ask what you're reading – you can tell them it's 'educational'.

Wicked

/wikid/ evil or morally wrong

Synonyms: evil, sinful, immoral . . .

To be fair, I don't agree with the whole definition, just the EVIL and MORALLY WRONG parts. LOL!

Oh, and I almost forgot to mention another reason why you have to get on the first bus, and this is taken directly from the School of Cool handbook written in 1983 (which was in the proper olden days, bruh).

> TO BE A REAL AND SEASONED SCHOOL BUS LEGEND, ONE MUST COMMAND AND CONQUER THE BACK SEATS OF THE BUS. FOR DOUBLE-DECKER BUSES, THIS MUST BE THE UPPER DECK. ONLY THEN WILL YOU BE RECOGNIZED AS AN OG.

But the forecast doesn't look good with this queue, my G. And remember, if you miss the first bus you're riding with the Famous Five. And securing those top-deck back seats simply ain't happening. I'll tell you what *will* happen though: you'll be smack-bang in the middle of the bottom deck with a bunch of old grannies or, even worse, next to a wild and out-of-control toddler who won't stop bouncing on their seat and ringing the bell.

Good news! The bus has arrived and it's almost empty, which means I'm not missing the first bus. The bad news is, I boarded at the end and am now sitting downstairs in GRANd Central next to an old lady called Mildred on one side (yep, she's already introduced herself), and a toddler (who's also introduced himself by wiping a fat booger on my leg). His name is Hunter, at least that's what the frantic adult that's with him is calling him as she desperately tries to stop him climbing out that tiny little slide window. Kid is agile, I'll give it to him. Hunter by name, hunter by nature too it looks like from the way he is eyeballing me. I genuinely think I'm his prey right now. Help!

Two stops to the weekend, two stops to the weekend. Two stops.

If I keep saying it, while I stare at Mildred's blue hair – which I kinda like by the way (#SWAG) – I'll get home quicker!

Oh yeah, forgot to say 'two stops' is why my mum lets me take the bus in the first place as it's only a 'short trip', and to prepare me for secondary school next year.

And look at that: it's my stop already! Whoop! Yep, that was quick I know, but hey, this is a book after all – sometimes speed limits don't apply.

Anyway, my house is the one with the yellow door. See, even my door blings! And it's number one too, which, as I think about the Royal Rap Rumble, strikes me as a good sign. Maybe I was born for this.

Finding my keys though, not so much. My fault as usual. Mum has always said, 'clip them to your trousers. That way you'll never lose them'. Yeah right, Mum. I might not lose them, granted, but I will lose my self-respect. And as a kid who KNOWS how to dress, I'll soon look like the school caretaker . . . and I don't mean that disrespectfully to our caretaker, Ray; he's a G when it comes to DIY and school stuff. But when it comes to SWAG, not so much.

Yet here I am, still searching the depths of my school bag for keys, proving that mums are always right. *WARNING* DO NOT TELL ANY MUM – EVER – THAT I SAID THAT! Even though it's true. I don't know how, man, but they're just always right. It's like an annoying superpower or something. **Arggggghhhhhh!** (Another scream of frustration!)

Aha! I think I found them! Oh no, that's just a chilli heatwave Dorito. What a touch though! Yum! And there are my keys too: they were hiding behind the crisp. LOL!

Now, one swift turn of these bad boys and the weekend begins: no school, no stress and no Bully Boy. So here goes!

I'm in!

'Ma, I'm home!'

'Is that you ▇▇▇▇▇? How was your day?' she yells back.

(Sorry, peeps, but for now we're still getting to know each other, so my government name will have to remain top secret. Identity theft is rife at the moment.)

'Yep! Just gonna go upstairs for a bit.'

'NO. YOU. ARE. **NOT**!'

Uh-oh, her voice changed volume with every word there. That's never a good sign.

And then she says those three words no kid ever wants to hear:

Busted! Mum's now emerged from the kitchen, wiping her hands on a tea towel. Honestly, these mums love a tea towel, don't they? They're rarely seen without them. Like a trusty little sidekick for all their mum needs.

'I can't believe you threw a book at a teacher and then tried to smoke her out of her classroom with your little skunk butt!'

Woah! This is more detail than I was expecting. Did Mr G dob me in? Surely not.

'They have even sent me a clip of the CCTV footage.'

Double **BUSTED!** I forgot they installed corridor CCTV after 'The Great Roast Potato Robbery' last year. You can read all about it online. The victim – Lil P (I strongly believe P now stands for Potato, not Pedro) from Year 4 – is still undergoing counselling to recover from the ordeal. According to him, he went to go and get some cheese and crackers from the salad bar to accompany his golden spuds and then WHOOSH, his roasties were gone! But then, that afternoon break the remains (those crunchy crispy bits – why would you leave those?) were found at the bottom of the school slide.

It must have been the crafty culprit's escape route. Then, after a lengthy line of questioning (we all had to miss Golden Time), they quickly realized no kid was gonna talk, so CCTV was installed to catch any future furtive felons.

PING! Idea: if we just stay silent maybe a superhero will show up and save us. What do you reckon?

.

.

.

(Awkward silence . . .)

.

.

.

(Even more of an awkward silence . . .)

71

Nope. No sign of a superhero, and I can also confirm that the ground has not swallowed me up either. This weekend is not starting well!

'You are grounded for two thousand, three hundred and eighty-six years, young man!'

I move to protest but she keeps going.

'Two thousand, three hundred and eighty-six years and eleven months, twenty-three days, seven hours, forty-two minutes and fifty-eight seconds.'

Two thousand, three hundred and eighty-six years and eleven months, twenty-three days, seven hours, forty-two minutes and fifty-eight seconds. Yep, my mum loves to exaggerate. Don't all mums and grown-ups?

Yes ☐

No ☐   (Also Yes)

Speaking of exaggerations. Here are some of my mum's greatest hits:

MUM'S GREATES

1. **I'VE TOLD YOU A MILLION TIMES…**
   Really? I mean, she's probably said stuff like 282,657 times yeah, but a million times? Hmmmmmm, bit much!

2. **IF YOU BREAK YOUR LEG, DON'T COMING RUNNING TO ME!**
   And how would I physically do that with a broken leg, Mum?

3. **I WASN'T BORN YESTERDAY, YOU KNOW!**
   Think we have all worked that one out by now, the grey hairs give it away!

4. **I'VE HAD IT UP TO HERE WITH YOU!**
   Where is 'here' exactly? I've always wanted to know. And what happens when the amount you've had it up to actually gets to 'here'? Has anyone survived?

5. **IF ALL OF YOUR FRIENDS JUMPED OFF A CLIFF, WOULD YOU?**
   Pretty sure this depends on where you are and who you're with. For example, if you're on a cliff-jumping holiday with friends who are both responsible and trustworthy (not people like Bully Boy or The Lads) and you have paid for an excursion to an idyllic cliff-jumping spot with fully-qualified professional guides, this makes total sense, no?

6. **IF YOU WATCH TOO MUCH TV YOUR EYES WILL TURN SQUARE!**
Surely they'd turn rectangular if they were going to turn any shape, Mum. TVs aren't square.

7. **EATING CARROTS WILL HELP YOU SEE IN THE DARK.**
So will a torch, or better yet turning on a light.

8. **WERE YOU BORN IN A BARN?**
Short answer: no. Longer answer: you were there, remember, Mum?

9. **I AM GOING TO COUNT TO THREE...**
Still waiting to find out what happens here, as I have never ever, ever, *ever* let her get to three. We got to two and three-quarters once . . . and I still don't like to talk about it.

10. **WE'LL SEE.**
With age, experience and great wisdom, I've come to learn that 'we'll see' quite simply means, 'this will never happen'!

Sorry for going off topic for a bit there but hey, it's kinda true, don't you think? In fact, if your mum has recorded her own compilation of Greatest Hits, jot them down below — you know, just to make yourself feel better. It helps, trust me!

Over to you, my G. I'll even help you out with the first track:

1. **DON'T MAKE ME REPEAT MYSELF!** (Without fail, she will . . . again and again and again!)

2.

3.

4.

5.

6.

7.

8.

9.

10.

Right, that's that then – when it's off your chest, you feel less stressed!

I've figured that in times like this, it's best to just go to bed. Think: if I go to sleep now, then Mumster the Monster might disappear by tomorrow morning, just like a dream. And then I can carry on with my weekend plan to begin prepping for rap domination.

Oh, and if YOU are reading this right now, at night, and you're already in bed, I guess this is perfect timing (and a sign) for you to switch your lamp or cool reading light off and catch some Zs too. Boogie sleep is a thing, you know. It's like beauty sleep but, on this occasion, the more you sleep the more you can boogie and buss a move – you know, cut some serious shapes on the dancefloor. We call that skankin' in my endz; so, yeah, big up all of my skankers! Oh, and the sleepers too.

Night, BROmigo!* And I'll see you in chapter 5.

*Sidenote 9: Forgot to say, if you're not reading this at night though and you're just on the bus, or in class, or maybe even on holiday somewhere, you don't have to go to sleep, okay? Just make sure you wake me up before the next chapter so I can explain what's happening. Cool!

CHAPTER 5

The Big Pick!

BEEP BEEEEEEP!

What's that sound?! Make it stop! Please!

Yep, I forgot to turn my alarm off, my G, and now I'm wide awake way too early for an S-Day. To make matters even worse, I've just remembered that I'm grounded too! I still can't believe Mum is making me stay home for the whole weekend. It's defo a weak-end now. (Get it, 'cause its weak. Ha!)

She hasn't always been like this. Mum, I mean. In fact, she used to be chilled and so much fun. The best in the

West and never ever ever ever ever stressed! (Sorry, but just had to make a point of how much of a ledge she was back in the day.)

But then Dad left. That's when everything changed. We won't go into that now though, 'cause it's bare depressing and I don't want to kill the mood, but just know that since then things have been really different. For starters, most of the time it just feels like it's me and my Lil Sis (who is proper annoying by the way) at home. I mean, Mum is there of course but she isn't at the same time, if you get me – proper distant. And that means that nowadays we only do things together as a fam on special occasions and that's super lame! And even on those days, Mum's kinda disconnected like her phone reception when it ain't got any bars. Not to get too emosh, but we really miss 'Fun Mum'. She was the best and so sick at so many cool things: especially Uno. Wowza! She'd win every single time. It was like she had the brain of Yoda, the speed of Spiderman and CR7's finish.

⟹ Not the vomit kind

Ha! Oh, and she was always so kind too! In fact, her favourite thing to say to us was, 'Cure them with kindness' every time we'd get wound up or upset by someone . . . or each other. See! So many happy memories and good times together! But then 'Fun Mum' became 'Glum Mum', and she's pretty much been like that ever since . . . well, for the past three years at least. I get it – I'm sad Dad left as well. And I suppose he was like 'her person' and then he was just gone. But she's sort of like 'my person', at least my adult one, and I wish we got to be more like we used to. I know she loves me and that, my G, but she hasn't even heard me spit my sick barz. She just ain't interested. What about you? What's your family situation like? In my experience (and that is my experience from observing at school), all families are different and that's pretty cool. So what kind do you have?

Look! There's goes my Lil Sis now with Pup Smoke, my dog. I am a rapper remember, and rappers have dogs, or should I say dawgs. Usually big dawgs! Grrrrrr!

The only issue: my dawg ain't no Bully, Staff or Rottie.
Nope! My dog, to be precise, is a Japanese Chin. A Japanese
Chin you're thinking, right? Thought so. Well, why don't
you take a few minutes to google it? I'll just chill here and
wait for you while you do.

(A few minutes later . . .)

Okay, now you're back let me have a guess at what you discovered about the Japanese Chin:

1. It's small and elegant (face palm) *Check!*

2. It's average height is between 20–28 centimeters (double face palm) *Check!*

3. It doesn't weigh more than a bag of flour (head in hands and shouts whhhhhyyyyy?!) *Check!*

Yep, you read that correctly: MY dog for MY **swagged-out** rap videos and career doesn't weigh more than a bag of flour. A bag of flour! How am I going to bring Pup Smoke down to my future music videos to look menacing, aye? Life really does suck right now: I'm grounded, my dog is basically a cat and now my annoying Lil Sis is sitting directly opposite me. How did she even get here? Swear she's a ninja! Can this get any more peak for me today?

'Grounded again are we, noodle neck?'

I guess the answer to that question is YES! See, at this point I know what she's after: a reaction. She wants me to lose my cool. Does your little sister, brother, cousin or mate do that to you, my G? Well, a reaction ain't happening today, my friend! Instead, I'm going to give her the poker face.

10/10 execution. Zero emotion and now she's annoyed, I can tell.

'Don't pretend you're happy with being sent your room for two thousand years! You'll have hair like Rapunzel by the end of your sentence, fuzzbutt!'

Okay, that was quite funny. A butt with fuzz. LOL! But not as funny as what I have planned for my comeback:

THE PICK 'n' FLICK!

The history of the Pick 'n' Flick is complex, and a source of much dispute among historians. Some say it was invented by the Ancient Romans, a strategy adopted by gladiators in the battle arena to distract an opponent. Others say it was first used by Tutankhamun in Ancient Egypt. It is thought the child Pharoah used it to annoy his siblings. After an analysis of the historical evidence, most historians now believe that the Pick 'n' Flick was invented by none other than the OG king of words, William Shakespeare. Turns out, creating 38 plays and 154 sonnets (that we know of) means a lot of writing. And sometimes writing can be a lonely business, my G. To overcome boredom, Will would pick 'n' flick at passersby to keep his mind entertained. Here are the steps if you want to join in with the fun too.

The Pick 'n' Flick Tutorial:

Step 1: Choose your strongest, most flexible, agile and reliable finger. If you're not sure which finger this is, practice makes perfect.

Step 2: Time to flare! This is when you use your nostril muscles to open the two holes at the end of your nose as wide as possible. I'm talking 'Grand Canyon' vibes!

Step 3: Dig deep. And I mean search far and wide, my friend. Think of yourself as a nose miner looking for your long-lost bogey buddy. Better yet, you're a bold and fearless explorer on a mission to retrieve the golden nugget. Except this nugget ain't gold — it's green, slimy, sticky, oozy and gooey.

Step 4: Once you've struck gold (or green), you have achieved stage one of this mission: THE PICK! Congrats! Now give yourself a pat on the back (but not with your bogey hand of course).

Step 5: It's time to create the perfect weight and shape of your mucus monster. This is called THE ROLL. And to achieve this masterful stroke, simply place your big fat booger between your index finger and thumb and then slowly start to roll. Back and forth, round and round!

Fun Fact: you will notice that the stickiness and snottiness of your nose goblin gradually evaporates and starts to form an outer crust. This is a sign of success, believe me! The harder the better, and the faster it flies!

So, how are you getting on, my G?

Smashing it ☐
Trashing it ☐

Hang in there either way. The next part is the important part!

Step 6: Once you have the perfect snot sphere, you are ready for THE FLICK. Place your snot rocket carefully on your thumb. Then slowly position your index finger tactically behind it. Once settled, slowly draw back that index finger. Yep, nice and slow. This is what I call the PRIME POSITION!

Now there's only two things left to do:

Step 7: Aim . . . (I usually close one eye at this point 'cause that's what they do in the movies).

Step 8: You can guess what's next, right? Target locked. Deep breath. One eye closed and . . .

'Ergh! What was that?' She is furious.

Mission accomplished.

RUUUUUUUUUUUUUUUUUNNNNNNNNN!

She's coming for me. Help me out, my G. Create a distraction: you know, make a noise or shout out 'OI!' really loudly!

'Ahhhhhhhhhhhhhhhhhhhhhhhhh!'

One thing about my sister is that when she has a bee in her bonnet there's no stopping her. And right now, this is bigger than a bee in her bonnet. This is more like a pterodactyl in her satchel. Yep, she is more vexed than a hungry T-Rex in an allotment! Fumin'!

'█e█, just stop!' she's pleading. I'm much faster than her so she can never catch me. But woah, that was close. And did you see what just happened there? She nearly revealed my real name to you. PHEW! She did give away one letter though: E. The question is: do you think you can work out the rest of the letters, my G? Well, if you fancy it, I've taken the liberty of giving you some lines below to have a few wild guesses. Yep, it's time to play 'The Name Game'.

____e_____

____e_____

____e_____

____e_____

____e_____

The good news is that now you have these written down, you can go back and check if you've guessed correctly later on in the book when, I mean, if, you ever do find out my real name. You never know!

Anyway, while she's still chasing me why don't I drop another rap? We've not had one for a while, and this feels like the perfect time to spit some home truths about Lil Sis, aka the bane of my existence! And you know the deal by now, join in if you fancy it, my G. Let's go!

Sister Blister

Did you know sister rhymes with blister?

It's not a coincidence!

And just like a blister I cannot shift her,

Whatever the incident!

Sunday to Saturday,

Jan to December,

She's always by my side.

But all blisters pop,

And that's when she stops,

Until our next big fight!

And there you have it, my Lil Sis summed up in a rap: she's annoying, she's irritating . . . but she's also kinda cute. Didn't expect me to say that, did ya, my G? Well, it's true. I think it's her big eyes, they make her look like one of those adorable Pixar characters. And the best bit: she's a bit of a wild child, which is challenging for me as a big brother, but also I can't help but respect it.

My Lil Sis knows what she wants and isn't afraid to ask for it. She's a future leader, I just know it. So does Mum. And, whatever happens between us, even though sometimes she's a blister, she's my blister. Urgh! That sounds weird, but you know what I mean – we're a team. Most of the time on the same side, but sometimes on opposite ones. We love each other A LOT. And we wind each other up A LOT! It's the sibling way. Do you get that with your sibling/s, family or best buddy?

Yay ☐
Nay ☐

Jeeeeez, I've spent waaay too much time chatting about my Lil Sis. Now I'm going to spend the rest of the day annoying her. Ha! That will make the time fly as fast as my future private jet on its way to the Grammys. Then, I'll only have twenty-four hours left stuck in Housecatraz (FYI: Alcatraz was a prison from the olden days on a giant rock out in the ocean so you couldn't escape). Then it's back to school to start Mission Cool: the birth of a rap duo like no other – Beatz 'n' Barz. So gassed for this and ready to roll, or should I say RAP!

Catch you tomorrow, my G.

P.S. If you managed to execute the Pick 'n' Flick perfectly, just know I'm proud of you, my G! Pick 'n' Flick Clique for life.

Laterz, BROda!

CHApTER 6

And Then We Rest . . .

Welcome to Sunday: the slowest day of the week. The day when nothing happens, ESPECIALLY when you're grounded. So, to avoid the awkward silence and snail-like journey to nowhere, let's just move on to chapter 7 already. Cool with you? Wicked!

See you tomorrow, BROnocchio!

CHAPTER 7

Now It's GO TIME

BEEP BEEEEEEP!

There goes the Rise 'n' Shine again, which can only mean one thing. I'm not grounded any more! Booya! Never thought I'd be so gassed for a Monday morning and to go to school. But hey, I am a kid on a mission after all, and the plan is as clear as a blingin' diamond on your favourite rapper's pinky:

- Get to school
- Sign up for the Rap Rumble auditions
- Win the auditions

- Enter the competition
- Win the competition
- Take over the world!

In that order specifically. Couldn't be clearer and couldn't be easier!

But first: breakfast. Apparently it is the most important meal of the day, and I can't help but agree. It sets you up with the energy you need for the day ahead and I'm proper hyped to to see what Mum has hooked up for me this morning – she's a bit of a masterchef in the kitchen you know . . . her spicy chicken is finger lickin'! And after the weekend I've had (or not had for that matter), I deserve a BIG breakfast treat. I reckon she feels really bad about being too hard on me on Friday. I'm guessing she has lovingly prepared some fresh protein pancakes (got to get them gains) swimming in a sea of sweet maple syrup. Peng! Or creamy, delicious Greek yoghurt sprinkled with crunchy granola and sweet chocolate chips. Bangin'! Actually, wait –

I know! It's obvious. She's making my favourite thing in the world CHUUUUUUURRRRROOOOOOOOSSSSS! Sounds even better when you say it with a DJ scratch thing at the beginning like this: Chicka chicka CHURROS!

Here, you have a go!

Repeat after me: chicka chicka churros!

To level-up some more just make the 'chicka chicka' bit high-pitched and do a DJ scratch hand at the same time. How did you get on? Smashed it, I bet!

Oh man, I just love churros. The crunch of their golden-brown exterior, straight into that soft doughy centre. OMD! I can't wait. In fact, let's go and get stuck into this FEAST.

'Mum! I'm coming in. What's for breakfast?'

'Oh just sit down and eat your porridge, N _ e _ _!' she says.

Woah, woah, woah! Rewind, come again, my selector! Did she just say **PORRIDGE?** AND give away another letter of my legal name at the same time?

What kind of joke is this?! Porridge! Do I look like Oliver Twist?

Please, sir, I DO NOT want ANY, let alone more!

'Why are you laughing?'

Why am I laughing? Because this must be a joke, surely. She's taking the Mickey, the Minnie, the Donald and the Daphne!

'Quick, eat up before it gets cold. Nobody likes cold porridge.'

She's got that right. Nobody likes porridge, hot or

cold!* There's something about the texture, my G. It just ain't for me. I'm out of here . . .

'I'll grab something from Breakfast Club, don't worry, Mum.'

'Fine! But please make sure you do.'

Phew, that was a close one.

*Sidenote 10: Sorry if you are a porridge eater, my G. No disrespect or anything – that slop just ain't my thing. I prefer to eat my food, not slurp it.

Right, back to the mission and we are fully focused. So much so, I think I'm seeing things, 'cause that looks like SFX at the bus stop. Wait a sec . . . it is her! I'm gonna chat to her: we are kinda friends now, after all.

'You cool, SFX?'

She points at her

jacket. This time to a different section and it reads, 'All good in the hood'. Sweet!

'How are you feeling about signing up for the Royal Rap Rumble?'

She points to 'Ready to roll' and then 'My G'. Can't lie, this is so cool. I know how hard it is to talk sometimes when you're feeling nervous — I get it — but the fact that she's found a way to communicate that suits her, I love it.

'Awesome! And now, how about dropping a beat? We can practice before the bus arrives.'

Gotta be honest with you, my freestyling is a little rusty but we gotta be a well-oiled machine if we're going to win this competition.

Her mouth opens. She's going to buss a sick beatbox live. Get ready to hit record, my G. This is gonna be epic! But what's she doing with her hand. It's like she's pointing behind me at something.

'Tap, please!'

Wow, I didn't realize SFX could do impressions too.

She sounds exactly like a middle-aged cockney geezer . . .
One sec: that's not SFX, it's Flat-cap Stanley, our bus
driver. I didn't even hear the bus pull up. That's why she
was pointing! LOL

'Chop chop, sunshine! We ain't got all day, son.'

He's right. Soon I'll be at school, and you know where
I'm going and what I'm doing first: office noticeboard
to sign my life away to superstardom, racks of cash, sick
garms and lit cars. Life could be worse, aye?

Oh wait . . . It is worse. Grime gave me detention
starting today, remember? And I'm already late for it! How
could I forget?

'You okay, Z?' It's SFX, she asks me shyly as she guides
me on to the bus.

For once, I don't actually care where I sit. Bigger chicken
(allow fish, fam) to fry and all that. Or maybe be fried in
this case.

I'm sitting down now and SFX has sat next to me. I tell
her all about how and why Grime gave me detention last

week and the fact that I completely forgot about it.

'Never mind hard-boiled, Grime is gonna be scrambled by the time I arrive!'

'Don't worry. I bet Mr G can help. He's cool. He'll just explain that we can't rehearse for Royal Rumble if you've got detention.'

'SFX, you're a genius! That's it.' I'm feeling better already.

SFX points to 'I know it' on her jacket and smiles. I love the way she uses different ways to communicate how she's feeling. Legend! It's hard to explain but her vibe and energy is just so on-point. Feels like I've known her for ages, or maybe in a past life. Do you ever get that feeling when you meet someone, my G? Whatever it is, we just click! I guess we make a really good team. A dream team, in fact!

Ah, I feel better already, and ready for the next chapter, literally!

See you at school, BROnaldo!

CHAPTER 8

Let's Sign It!

Back at school, and I'm too nervous to face Grime so I've decided to run like a kid does from broccoli straight to Mr G's classroom in the hope that he's arrived already. Who knows, maybe his mum made him churros for breakfast instead of porridge and he's still at the breakfast table, munching on those. I wouldn't blame him.

I've made it (out of breath, may I add) and I've startled Mr G who is sitting at his desk, writing in his own Book of Raps. See, I told you: such a G!

'Z, What are you doing here so early?'

He looks proper confused right now!

'And Essef as well. Glad to see you're both getting along though.' I look behind me and SFX is in the doorway, quietly waiting for me. We've only known each other since Friday and she's already got my back. That's a true friend, my G.

'Mr G, I forgot that Grime gave me detention last week, starting this morning. What should I do?'

'Don't worry, Z. I explained to Mr Grimewood that you didn't throw the book at Mrs Malinki. You don't have to go to detention.'

Booya! What a relief, my G! We are free!

'Wow, thanks, Mr G. I owe you one.'

'Once you've signed up for the Royal Rap Rumble, we can call it even, Z. The sign-up form is outside the assembly hall. Now go and change the world, kid.'

Walk with me, my G.

Exactly 6.5 minutes later. The amount of time it takes to walk from Mr G's room to the assembly hall . . .

There it is in all its glory: the world-renowned logo and the pièce de résistance (that's French for 'the best thing since sliced bread') for all rap worshippers around the world, THE GOLDEN MIC. I'll say that again, homie: THE GOLDEN MIC!

Which means there's only one thing left to do – swagger walk on over and add our name to the sheet: Beatz 'n' Barz! Easy peasy lemon Yeezys! It's going to be one small step for us; one giant leap for rapkind. And we are so ready for this. Yep, we're doin' it, my G. We're signing up.

We're gonna change the WORLD!

Okay, deep breath . . . Woooooooooossssaaaaaaaa!

You can take a deep breath too . . .

And here we go——

'Not so fast, likkle boy!'

Urgh! Not again! Yep, that's the sound of Bully Boy's voice. Honestly, this boy is like one of those annoying wasps in the summer – you know the kind that just keeps coming back no matter what you do!

'How are you going to sign up to the Rap Rumble, deadbeat. You can't even speak!'

As per usual, his meerkat-like mandem start joining in with high-pitched laughs and their random pointing routine, bumping into each other and then laughing. They remind me of those evil hyenas in *The Lion King*. I'm not responding. It's not worth it.

But wait! They've suddenly stopped. Now they're leaning in, whispering to each other as they move closer. My eyes are mostly closed at this point, ready for impact, as if Bully Boy is about to strike, but . . . nothing happens.

Suddenly there is a sharp intake of breath and people in the background are chuckling under their breath. I open my eyes and see SFX pointing to a phrase on the back of her jacket. Bully Boy and his homies have started to back away. SFX is now smiling at me and that's when I see what it says: 'I'd insult you, but you're probably too slow to get it anyway!'

If I had a mic, I'd give it to SFX right now so she could drop it. Ratings! She reminds me of Lil Sis a bit – never backs down, especially when it comes to a bully.

We take a moment to do our standard 'we smashed it' air spud (that's a non-contact fist bump by the way) and then we walk off into the distance like they do at the end of a movie. I won't lie. My head is a little higher than it normally is walking away from Bully Boy. We'll come back later when they've gone to add our names to the list. Then we'll win the whole thing and our name will be in lights just like this:

BEATZ 'N' BARZ

This incident with Bully Boy is just a blip in the rap road. It's a minor not a major, my G. We have to keep moving forwards, and usually a step in the right direction involves Mr G.

'Shall we go see what Mr G is saying, SFX?'

She points to her shoulder this time and it reads 'All gravy!'. That means everything's calm. You know, cool, aka all good.*

Sidenote 11: I love gravy, do you?
Especially on chips – that slaps!

Speaking of gravy and food, I need to grab a slice of toast from Breakfast Club first 'cause my belly is rum-b-ling! And allow going into lessons more Hungary than Budapest (Get it? It's the capital of the country Hungary), 'cause then you're setting yourself up for a silent strike. And when hunger strikes, especially in the middle of 'big write' or 'hot task', it sounds like a megalodon doing the tango with a triceratops in your loft in the middle of the night. Anyway, you get my point . . . let's munch! Breakfast Club is in the canteen, follow me!

Mmmmmm! I can smell the toast before I can see it. And speaking of toast, what's your favourite toast topping? Rank your favourite spread below. One being your favourite and five being your Marmite. Most kids think that stuff is minging! Over to you . . .

Butter ☐   Jam ☐   Marmite ☐
Peanut Butter ☐   Honey ☐

Glad we got that sorted. To be honest with you, I have a mature pallet and I'm used to the finer things in life, so I'd probably go for a piece of fresh seeded sourdough with egg whites and avocado. Oh, and a light dusting of chilli flakes — caviar, if I'm feeling proper bougie! But that ain't happening in this gaff, no way! So today I'm choosing the classic 'utter butter' option. Sometimes you gotta keep it simple and stay humble, my G.

Anyway, school starts at 08:40 but we aren't registered until 08:50 and the time now is 08:47. I can't let SFX be late on her first Monday at a new school after she's already come through for me so much today. If we take a short cut through Ray's office (the caretaker, remember?) and then buss a quick right (like a ninja) past Grime's doom room, then we can get to the Rap Rumble sign-up sheet, sign it and then, head to class before you can say 'boom shacka lack'.

'You ready, SFX?'

I wait for her to point to her jacket but instead she raises an eyebrow and says, 'Let's GO!'

And we're off. First the short cut, and it's light work. Piece of cake! Now it's ninja time. **Shhhhhhhhhhhhhhhhhhhh!**

Swift and silent. That's how we roll.

Time for the snapbacks. That way no one will see our bait faces. Okay, and the hats are on, peak down low. Time to shimmy and shuffle past you know where. Slowly does it. Aight, and we're cool.

Time to sign the sheet and then dash to class, but WAIT!

'Ermmm, where's the Rap Rumble sign-up sheet?'

'Say Whhhaaattt!' SFX responds.

BREAKING NEWS, MY G! It's gone. Yep, the Rap Rumble sign-up sheet is nowhere to be seen. The same goes for my dream. I'm heartbroken, and fartbroken (this is when you're so heartbroken you let out a squeaky sad fart). The journey is over, my G. Another dead end!

Whyyyyyyyyyyyyyyyyyyyyyyyyyyyyyyyyy????????!!!!!!!

I think I need a moment.

.

.

.

Sorry, that was me just going through the (e)motions. Gotta let the feelz out sometimes, you know?

Wish I could stay with you, so we can chat about this a bit more, but I've got to get back for registration. Can't believe the adventure is over. :(

Maybe see you in the next chapter, or maybe not, I guess? Whatever happens, thanks for rolling me with this far, my G.

See ya, BRO-na Lisa!

CHAPTER 9

Plan B: We've Gotta Find It!

'Z?'

Phew. That was close! But it's all good in the hood; we've made it just in time for the register. Mrs Malinki is clearly still upset about last Friday because she is throwing me some serious daggers with her eyes! But not the standard daggers you throw when you're annoyed. These are on another level. Put it this way, you know that sword that got stuck in the stone in that olden-day story – the impossible one that King Arthur pulled out to become king? Well, times its sharpness by infinity, then mix it with a Great White Shark's bite and an out-of-control possessed chainsaw, and that's how sharp her stare is.

Man, does she hold a grudge! In the words of Elsa, 'Let it go, fam!' Well, not the 'fam' bit, but you know what I mean.

Warning: Brain wave! Actually, Elsa, if you're reading this, I'm down for a remix of your movie anytime. I've even got the name sorted. You ready for it? Drumroll, please . . .

3 . . .

2 . . .

1 . . .

BROzen!

Now that's what you call a Hollywood blockbuster!

Anyway, I'm getting distracted. There goes the brain SPLASH again!

You're still here though, my G?

Yes ☐

I didn't put a no box, because if you're not here how are you going to tick it? Durrrr!

Anyway, back to the plan, and the question remains: Where did the sign-up sheet go? Two more questions to add in fact: Who took it? And where did they put it?

I can see that SFX is clearly thinking what I'm thinking. Yep, those two words that taste more sour than a packet of Toxic Waste sweets rolled in lemon juice and then dipped in vinegar: Bully Boy! I bet he's got it stashed away in his school bag.

Why didn't I clock that before? Of course he took it! It is such a Bully Boy thing to do.

The good news: he's sitting on the table behind me.

The bad news: I don't fancy eating a knuckle sandwich for lunch, with a glass of orange squash(ed) head, so I have to be super tactical if I am going to get it back. I smell a secret mission, my G. And do you know what every secret mission needs? An epic plan.

We keep our school bags outside of the classroom in the corridor on pegs. The problem is, you're not allowed to leave the class unless you have a . . . remember? Yep, a toilet permit, or as I like to call it, a poo-pee pass. So that's step one sorted, it's time for a desperate urge for the loo to earn the backstage access-all-areas pass, and I'm going for it. But be prepared, as this is going to be dramatic.

Here we go:

Step 1: The shoe shuffle. Start slow and then get faster and faster and faster to gain attention. Objective met: people are looking.

Step 2: It's time for the chair bounce. Let's do this! Granted, visually this looks a bit weird but it is the universal sign for 'I need a wee' and it's working!

Mrs Malinki's now looking at me, and she's about to say something. Oh, please let it be true. Those sweet, sweet words. I can see them climbing out of her mouth as we speak.

'Oh, go and use the toilet, Z, before you have an accident.'

Bingo bango, I could tango with a mango! I am free, my G. The plan is well underway, so now it's time to hit the corridor. I bet those pegs have been pegs-pecting me! Ha! Get it? That's what you call a peg-cellant pun. Woo hoo! Okay okay, no more – I feel peg-hausted! LOL! Okay, let's get serious. I've got about four minutes at the most before Mrs Malinki sends someone looking for me.

Step 3: We need to locate Bully Boy's bag.

Of course I could look at the names above the pegs, but all I really need to do is sniff. Bully Boy loves a cheap cologne. You know the type that is always sold with an accompanying body wash. Yep, that stuff! The type that usually has a random WXYZ-lister celebrity on the front riding a horse or staring weirdly into your eyes – that's the scent, or should I say stench, we are searching for. I can smell it, and I can see the bag. Booya!

Step 4: Simple. Open the bag.

Approach with caution. Why? Because this bag has zips, clips, buttons, poppers and around fifteen keyrings attached to it. That's a lot of noise potential, my G, so we have to take this bit nice and slow. First the keyrings. Done! Now the front zip pockets – easy! But there's nothing in there. Okay, one final step: the clip, popper and big button. Nothing in there either.

'Can't find what you're looking for?'

I shake my head.

Wait a second: who said that?

Uh-oh! That's Bully Boy's voice!

Oh no. Caught red-handed. I literally have no excuse here. It's over! AGAIN! I'm DEADly serious this time. We've come to the end of the road, my G. Yep, but this time it's not the adventure that's over, it's me. I am LITERALLY about to DIE and considering you're the last person on Earth I'm speaking to before I go, I need you to pass on a few messages for me. I promise to keep it short and sweet, since I don't have long. Here we go:

1. Please tell my mum that I won't be home for dinner 'cause I have been crushed and then ripped into smithereens by a bozo Neanderthal.

2. Please tell my sister that now I am dead I can confirm that she's the most annoying person on Earth AND BEYOND.

3. Please tell Siri to add a free ice cream feature for all children in time for my next life and return to planet Earth.

4. Please tell David Attenborough to watch the CCTV footage of me perishing and to narrate it. My demise and passing will at least sound cool then.

5. And finally, please tell the dude who invented peri-peri chicken that I am very grateful for him being born and for bringing so much joy to me and my belly.

Okay, that's that then. Time to die. Goodbye!

((((GONG!))))

Saved by the bell, or should I say gong! And yes, that sound means my trusty warrior and worrier are here to help me work through my options:

THE TICKLE PICKLE

WARRIOR:

All you have to do is pretend you have a pickle in your hand. To do this, place your finger deep in your hand and wiggle it like a little pickle. You can even draw a smiley face on it if you want. Pickle fans will go wild here! And if the villain in question doesn't like pickles, they will still be interested to see a magical pickle randomly wriggling in your hand. Next, as they come in closer to check out the eighth wonder of the world, you take that pickle (your strongest finger) and then tickle them directly and wildly under their arm, smack-bang in the armpit zone. You can even say 'tickle tickle tickle' in a really high-pitched voice for effect. You can do it!

WORRIER:

Errmm, are you forgetting that you are 1.3M tall and Bully Boy is 1.6M, which means you are going to have to jump really high to successfully achieve this feat. And even if you do manage it, the likelihood of you not pulling a hamstring, beefstring or chickenstring is super slim. Meaning, this is not a good option at all. Plus it's super weird to just randomly tickle someone and not okay. So DON'T DO IT!

THE HOUDINI

WARRIOR:

This has been attempted only three times in the history of mankind and requires a greater element of surprise than you have now, but you have one hunderd per cent got this. It's simple: first, you have to throw something up in the air. Then, as soon as he looks up, just dart like a bullet through his legs and disappear like magic. Alakazam, my man!

WORRIER:

Abracada-BRUH, are you crazy? First of all, you have nothing to throw, and secondly he is standing in front of a wall, which means unless you are a rhino that has just bathed in Lucozade and coffee, and you are ready to charge through the wall, this plan is a solid fat fail!

THE WEDGIE

WARRIOR:

Ah, the oldest trick in the book and the actual move Theseus used on the minotaur back in the days of Ancient Greece. It's the world's best-kept secret and the choice of many famous world conquerors: Julius Caesar, Napoleon Bonaparte, Atilla the Hun, Alexander the Great and King Leonidas from the Spartans, you name them and they used it. Don't believe any of that other mythical nonsense you have read or heard, the wedgie has been the go-to GOAT move FOR EVER. And for me, this is the only option you have: it's easy to deliver, doesn't require much strength and the damage is so effective, you buy yourself a good amount of time to flee. Oh, and the steps are simple:

- Go in for the apology hug.
- When they accept your gesture of kindness, you—

WORRIER:

Don't say another word! You do realize if you do this, you're going to get in massive trouble not just with Bully Boy but also every person of power in the school. Detention, suspension, or maybe expulsion, which are all worse than your bleak future. So, whatever you do: DON'T DO THIS! Cure them with kindness, remember? Oh, and mums are ALWAYS right!

Oh man, why does this have to be so hard, my G. I mean, what would you do?

Tick below:

The Tickle Pickle	☐
The Houdini	☐
The Wedgie	☐
None of the above	☐

Tough decision, innit? Hmmmmm. I've decided to go for the 'Tickle Pickle'. It seems like the only logical option, to be fair. Wish me luck and just dill (a pickle pun) with it! LOL. Let's GO!

'Erm, what are you doing, you weirdo?'

I think it's working. I'm getting closer, he looks confused, and he's staring at the pickle. Time to give it a wiggle!

'Wait, what is in your hand?'

I'm really close now. I can see the armpit. It's nearly time to unleash the pickle, my G.

'This is so weird, dude!'

One more step!

'Hey, is that supposed to be a pickle?'

And . . . ACTION!

'HA HA HA HA HA HA HA HA HA HA HA HA HA HA!!!'

It's working! The pickling is tickling, and he's loving it! I just have to run now and I am free! Uh oh! Slight problem. I can't leave. My feet are like cement and I'm stuck. The thing is, I know exactly why: 'cause I'm actually having a lot of fun, and his laugh is now making me laugh too!

'HA HA HA HA HA HA HA HA HA HA HA HA HA HA HA!!'

'Aha Aha Aha Aha Aha Aha Aha Aha Aha Aha Aha Aha Aha Aha Aha Aha!!!'

You have to try this, my G! Seriously, a world with tickle pickles would be a better place, trust me! I've actually forgotten about the fact that I don't even like Bully Boy! It's magic! I vote Tickle Pickle for president! Tickle Pickle for prime minister! Tickle pickle for mayor! Tickle Pickle for eeeeevvvvvveeeerrrrr! Seriously though, can you imagine if we had a Tickle Pickle for every serious dispute across the world? There would be world peace in seconds! Here's some more tricky debates the Tickle Pickle would instantly solve:

Messi vs Ronaldo = Tickle Pickle

Michael Jordon vs Lebron James = Tickle Pickle

Minecraft vs Fortnite = Tickle Pickle

Candy vs Chocolate = Tickle Pickle

IOS vs Android = Tickle Pickle

Xbox vs PS = Tickle Pickle

Marvel vs DC = Tickle Pickle

Star Wars vs Star Trek = Tickle Pickle

Hotdogs vs Hamburgers = Tickle Pickle

And the biggest debate of them all. The one everyone in the world just can't seem to agree on: Pineapple on pizza, yes or no?

And the answer is: **TICKLE PICKLE!**

See, and with all of our problems solved, the world would be a better place!

Anyway, while you think about your next brilliant use of the Tickle Pickle, I'm going to get back to the tickling, or should I say pickling? LOL!

Warning: Brain Wave! If this takes off, we can even make our own Tickle Pickle merch. Picture this: a green finger sleeve with a smiley face and we're septillionaires! (That's a billion times a quadrillionaire, by the way.)

'Uh hum!'

It's Mr G.

'Z, what are you two doing?'

How do I explain this one? Seriously, how? Or do I just Tickle Pickle Mr G too? You never know. It might work! Actually, scrap that – that's kinda weird!

'Nothing, sir. I'm just going to the toilet, see ya!'

Oh, man, Bully Boy got in there first. And he's gone! Now what do I do?

'Nevermind! I've been looking for you, Z.'

He has? Why?

'There were only a couple of spaces left on the Royal Rap Rumble sign-up sheet so I took it down this morning for you and SFX to sign.'

No WAY! Mr G had the sign-up sheet the whole time! That means all of this was for nothing! Well, not nothing – we have discovered the world's next billion-dollar idea, but still.

'Auditions are on Wednesday, Z, so are you going to

sign up, or not?'

SNM, follow me, my G! It's time to SIGN!

3

2

1

And we're in! Beatz 'n' Barz are coming to a rap battle near you soon! Oh, and you're coming too, my G, remember? So make sure you sign on the dotted line below:

. . . .

SIGNED, SEALED, DELIVERED!

'Brilliant, now get back to class, Z.'

Ta-da! And we're back in class already! See, I told you books are magic. But wait, there is one problem . . . now I'm back in class I actually do need a wee. Help me, BROseph!

CHAPTER 10

Bad Rhyming or Bad Timing!

Chapter ten and I'm still holding my wee! Time really does go slow when you need to go. In fact, if today goes any slower it wouldn't surprise me if a bunch of sloths and snails start marching the streets with placards and megaphones complaining about the pace. Proper sluggish!

Anyway, the good news is that Mr G wants to see me and SFX in his room after school. Hopefully, it's for our first official rap practice. That would be epic! In fact, why don't we – with the power of book magic again – just speed things up, skip all of this boring class stuff and just get straight to the good bit? But, I am going to need your help, my G. These symbols below are old-skool boombox buttons. And here's what you need to do to get us to boot camp: First, press pause. Then, when you are ready to roll (and rap), hit and hold down the fast-forward button. About five seconds should be just the right amount of time to get to the end of the school day. And then press the play button. That's how they used play music in the olden days, my G. My mum loves the classics, she has an ancient stereo at home where she listens to things called cassettes and CDs.

Oh, and don't forget to crank the volume up! This one's gonna be vibez, bruh! Over to you!

Boom! We did it. We're in Mr G's classroom now (and I don't need a wee any more – hmmmmm, that must have been taken care of in super speed. LOL). And I was right: RAP BOOT CAMP begins!

'Yeseree, Z and SFX! It's time for you two to shine!'

Awesome! I wonder what we're doing first? I trust Mr G, so whatever it is I'm sure it's going to be proper epic!

'Our first challenge is the "Freestyle Flow"! All you have to do is pick three random cards from the set below and rap about them. And don't give me that salty look, Z, 'cause if you want to be the dankest rapper who's bussin on the microphone slaying it all day every day, you gotta be able freestyle! No cap!'

ONE: since when did Mr G start chatting like he goes to school here rather than teaches here? And TWO: I'm not a freestyler!

Mr G's now holding a bunch of cards and presenting them to the two of us.

'Let's do this!'

SFX picks three and then I pick three.

Great! I've got these dead words:

| Wolf | Silver | Chimney |

And the reason they are dead is because NOTHING rhymes with them! Don't believe me? Have a go yourself, my G! Done? See, I told you! It's impossible and I ain't doing it. SFX clearly feels the same too, as she's pointing to 'Hell to the NAH!' on her jacket.

'Your attitude determines your altitude, guys. Please believe in yourselves a little more and you can achieve anything!'

'I know we can, Mr G, but can we at least start with something that's a little easier?'

'No biggy, Z, let's move on to our second challenge.'

Yeah, good idea, sir! He takes the cards from us, then whips out something new . . . more word cards. PEAK!

'Now, the next challenge', says Mr G, 'is called "The Lyric Jumble". The rules are simple: All you have to do is use these words to make any rap lyric. Go for it!'

rap	I	future	god	bright	is	am
my	not	never	will	be	and	a

Hmmmm. This is tricky. You got anything, my G? I look
at SFX and she just shrugs her shoulders. PING! AHA! I've
got it!

'My future is not bright and I will never be a rap god!'

Harsh! I look at Mr G and SFX with worried eyes.

'Ouch!' Mr G says in a consoling voice. 'Hard luck that
time, Z! I was hoping you'd say, "I am a rap god and my future
is bright!" but, hey, you know what, that's why reading and
writing is so important. The more you love words, the
more they'll love you back. Soon you'll be feeling fine and
spitting rhymes. It just takes a bit of practice!'

'I bet he's right,' says SFX with a slick smile beaming
from her pearly whites. Mr G smiles too, probs because
SFX chose to talk in front of him, but he doesn't say

137

anything in case he makes her feel self-conscious.

'Let's try our final challenge,' says Mr G with fresh energy. 'It's called "The Word Bank". This one is really cool! All you have to do is choose a determiner, an adjective and a noun by rolling the dice.'

SFX and I look at him like he's trying to teach us something.

'Mr G, we're not in class.'

'It's fun, I promise! Each number on the dice connects to a word in each group, get it? You roll three times in total. And then you use the words to start forming super-cool phrases to use in your future raps. Sound like a plan?'

Determiner? Adjective? Noun? I'm starting to think the G in Mr G stands for grammar, LOL! Can you imagine that? Mr Grammar, LOL! Better yet: MC Grammar. Yeah, really see that one working! NOT! Hmmmmm! Anyway, let's give this a go. And you can play too, my G!

- Grab a dice
- Roll it once: whatever number you land on, find the numbered word in the list
- Do this two more times for the adjective and noun and you're good to go!

Here are the Word Banks:

Determiners	Adjectives	Nouns
1. The	1. chosen	1. one
2. One	2. dark	2. words
3. My	3. wicked	3. day
4. His	4. icy	4. king/queen
5. Her	5. blazing	5. gem
6. Their	6. untamed	6. beast

How did you get on, my G? Guess what I got? 4, 2 and 3, which comes together to make . . .

His dark day!

Great! I'm starting to think twice about the audition now, my G. Everything is feeling so negative and it ain't working for me. And, to make matters worse, Bully Boy has now somehow managed to get on the school PA system (which broadcasts absolutely everywhere, may I add) and is rapping about ME! I wanna cover my ears but my inner warrior always says you gotta know your enemy's strengths and weaknesses.

Bully Boy's Back!
My name's Bully Boy,
And I am a beast.
A predator,
Ready for a feast.
Sharp nails,
Sharp teeth.
Always on the hunt looking for beef!
With Z,
'Cause he's weak!

He can't rap,
He can't even speak!
He's a joke,
With a lump in his throat!
And who am I?
I'm the GOAT!

I can hear echoes of laughter from down the corridor. Mr G and SFX look at me with nervous faces.

I've decided to take this as a sign. Sometimes you just have to admit that it ain't your day, and today is SO not for me, my G. The good news is Mr G has said we can come back tomorrow morning before school and try again. Sorted!

See you tomorrow, BROtato! Nice and early! Not early worm early though – we all know what happens there, don't we?!

CHAPTER 11

Let's Warm Up!

It's the next day and it is time to get serious. SFX and I need your help, my G. We're trying to write a sick audition rap. We know if we get the rhymes tight then the rest will be easy peasy lemon Yeezys, but we need inspiration! And what's the best way to get inspiration for a new rap? To have a look in my Book of Raps and see some of the genius barz I've written in the past, of course!

Page sixteen: ah, this one's a banger!

The Pizza Rap!

This is a rap about pizza,

And it can't be topped.

That's why I cheese the day,

'Cause there ain't mushroom at the top!

That's right: I knead it!

Thin crust or deep dish,

Wanna hear a pizza joke?

Nah that's cheesy!

No no no, wait! Page twenty-eight:

The Chicken Rap!

This is a rap about chickens,

So if you're EGGSpecting,

For me to be a one-CHICK pony . . .

Bad CLUCK bro, I'm EGGcellent!

I've got HENdurance,

I am PECKtacular . . .

Other MCS get SCRAMBLED!

So you can call me SPATULA!

Scrap that! This is the one. Page sixty-three:

This Little Piggy

This little piggy played Fortnite.

This little piggy watched YouTube.

This little piggy bought Roblox.

This little piggy did a TikTok.

What happened to the other little piggy?

Not sure, but do you want some of this

bacon sandwich?

*Disclaimer: No pigs were harmed in the making of this rap.

Piggy promise! Just a joke – I don't even eat bacon, bro!*

Actually, all of these are too jokey. We want to be taken

seriously and write a rap that will BLOW the judges away.

Ha! BLOW THEM AWAY. Pardon the pun, but do you smell

another joke here? Actually, allow it. No more jokes about farting. We've done that now and to be honest it's getting kinda rude and immature of me. Next time I'll just do one about burping instead, LOL!

Anyway, here is what I am thinking. A couple of ideas that will surely lead to rap battle domination, and Beatz 'n' Bars becoming the GOAT as planned.

Scenario 1:

We audition and, just as the judges are about to make their big decision, I summon from the depths of my belly the biggest, loudest and proudest BURP ever! So powerful it creates a BURPquake, shaking the ground and their

brains as they hold on for dear life until they eventually give up and are literally blown away. BURP-fect timing because by the time they come around, they will be so confused and dazed they'll have no choice but to put us through! Genius!

Scenario 2:

We sprinkle a smidge (well, maybe a heap actually) of freshly cracked pepper on the judge's microphones so it gets sucked into their noses like a hoover when they breathe in. This will make them sneeze so much that they'll catch a case of amSNEEZEsia, which basically means they will lose all of their memories, and then ask me who won, and I'll just say we did! Double LOL LOL!

Brain wave! Actually, while we're on the subject of sneezes, here's two funny sneeze jokes and one riddle to make you chuckle.

Sneeze Jokes:

1. What's made of leather and sounds like a sneeze?
2. What sound does a nut make when it sneezes?

Sneeze Riddle:

If I am black I am clean. If I am white I am dirty. And if you get too close, you might sneeze. What am I?

Wondering where the answers are, my G? Just go to the back page of the book, flip it upside down and the truth will be revealed. Go on, off you go!

'Z, you're not taking this seriously,' says SFX, looking worried. I know that she wants the glory of lifting the Golden Mic trophy as much as I do, but sometimes it's fun to just joke around a bit. Do you agree, my G? Actually, maybe I should be a bit more mindful. After all, this is more than just a rap battle (for both of us) – it's about showing those haterz that you don't have to talk all the time to be a musical legend. You can be different. You can be YOUnique. YOU can be YOU!

'We need to get serious. Now.' she says, as she points to the 'Seriously' tag on her jacket.

She's right! We need something BIG here. Literally the best rap I've ever written. No pressure. Universe, help me! Pleeeeeeeeaaaaaaaaasssssssseeeeeee! Can you hear me? Hello, is anyone there?

.

.

.

(Phone ringing)

That's a positive sign!

Me: Hello, Universe, are you there?

Universe: Please hold the line. We are experiencing high demand on the Universe Manifestation Line at the present time. Please try again later.

Great. Even the universe can't help me!

SFX ain't bothered either. She's quietly started to practice her beats. They're all lit and I know one of them will inspire something great. Hmmmmm. Maybe I should meditate. That's what they do in all of the martial arts movies when they are searching for answers, or for the meaning of life. And if it's good enough for Po and Master Shifu, it's good enough for me. It looks pretty easy. You ready?

Let's do it!

Welcome to Meditation Class 101:

First of all, you need a clear space on your floor. Like properly clear. Don't just push all your mess to the corner. Cluttered floor, cluttered mind. That's why you should keep your bedroom clean, my G. (Or that's what my mum tells me anyway.) Done that? Cool, here are the steps:

Step 1: Cross your legs, like back in the day when you were in reception class, sitting on the carpet

Step 2: Do that thing that all the yogis do. You know, when you make two mini raptors with your hands and then point them towards the ceiling

Step 3: Close your eyes

Step 4: Take a deep breath

Step 5: Make your best 'Ohmmmmm' sound

Step 6: And now we wait!

.

.

.

.

Psstttttt. You getting anything?

.

.

.

.

.

Nope, me neither. I guess we just keep waiting.

.

.

.

.

Well look at that, I seem to have meditated (waited) so long the whole school day has disappeared (result!), along with the bus journey home, and we're already back at my yard! What a touch! The only problem is, it looks like I've lost SFX somewhere along the way. We can't have that, my G, as we still have loads of practice to do before the audition. And I've still got to figure out what I am going to rap about! Will you help me call her back? After three, let's shout SFX really loud.

Disclaimer: If you're somewhere super quiet like a library (sickest place) or in class, you can just close the book and come back when you're ready to shout. You ready?

1 . . . 2 . . . 3 . . .

SFX!

It worked! She must have been chatting to Lil Sis or playing with Pup Smoke.

That's the best thing about writing your own book: YOU decide how things turn out. (Well, not you, me. LOL.) And now SFX is back, we can get back to it. Yep, it's time for uni-VERSE-ity aka The FLOW Factory aka The Lyric Lab aka S'COOL! See what I did there? I just made school cool. Booya!

First: The bea— 'ESSEF!'

Woah, woah. Who is that interrupting our flow?

'Yes, Mum?'

Ohhhhhhh. Its SFX's mum. Now I see where she gets her voice from.

'Are you okay?'

'Yes, Ma! Sorry, Z, Mum is here too. She wanted to meet your mum, so she's come in for a cup of tea!'

'Thats cool! There's no way they are joining our crew though.'

'No way!' SFX agrees.

Sorted. Now, where were we, my G? Ah! The beat! We need something bangin' here. Something with bass and pace that will mashup the place! Cue SFX. She brings her hands to her mouth, opens wide and launches into some of the sickest sounds I've ever heard. Put it this way, if beats were chocolates what SFX has just dropped would easily be one those fancy shiny red balls you get at Christmas, or better still, the golden ones with the oozy chocolate hazelnut centre. She is my partner in CRHYME and every sound that comes out of her mouth is giving me the sickest and freshest ideas. The words are bubbling, ready to explode. And this time there ain't a fart or burp in sight, LOL!

The beat is lit and I am ready to spit. But first I need to get warmed up, and here's an important part of my process: tongue-twisters. They are a wicked way for you to work on your timing, flow, diction (how well you pronounce something) and speed. Have a look at these tongue twisters:

Easy:
She sells sea shells on the sea shore!

Intermediate:

How much wood would a woodchuck chuck if a woodchuck could chuck wood?

Advanced:

Betty Botter bought some butter, but she said the butter's bitter. And if I put it in my batter, it will make my batter bitter. But a bit of better butter will make my batter better. So Betty Botter went and bought a bit of better butter!

As you can see there are three levels. All you have to do is rap them on a beat. It is the perfect warm up. And the better you get, the faster you rap! Oh, and don't be too put off, my G. If you can't do it first time, have another go, and then another. Just don't stop! Look, even the word

IMPOSSIBLE

has the words

I'M POSSIBLE in it.

It all comes down to perception, and that just means how you see things. Take the word 'listen', for example. If you look at it carefully for long enough, you can make another word, 'silent', by rearranging the letters.

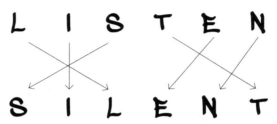

The moral: you have to be silent to truly listen. Not that that worked earlier during our meditation phase, but you know what I mean.

And that's it! We are warmed up and ready to rap. Hmmmm, but there's one small problem: I still don't know what to rap about! It's like I've got rapper's block.

'Try freestyling, Z,' SFX manages to yell in the middle of a beatbox. 'See what happens.'

She points to a tag on her jacket: 'JUST DO IT!'

She's right. I'm just gonna do it. We know that nerves

make me rhyme. So does talking in front of people and big crowds. And what's happening tomorrow? I am RHYMING (well, rapping) in front of people (big, serious judges from the biggest and sickest rap competition in the world) and a big crowd. And yes, there will be nerves. Lots of them. But, hey, I just have to lean into the nerves – and turn a negative into a positive. That's it! And it's working, my G. I'm actually freestyling! Just words start coming out first. None of them make much sense, but I am going with it and SFX is nodding in support. I'm finding my rhymes and everything is starting to flow. Now we have the lyrical lava bubbling and I'm on fire! Even Lil Sis has come to listen, and she's proper bopping her head like her neck is a slinky as the words explode out of my mouth. We're flowing, my G! It's taken me ten years to realize, but what I thought was a curse actually is a gift. My gift! My talent! And it is even better that I got to realize this with my ultimate musical G, SFX, by my side – and YOU, of course!

'Go, N_ek _,' cheers Lil Sis as she dances around us.

This is it. Tomorrow is our moment, and I am so gassed right now! I bet you're gassed too, my G? Of course you are! We're in this together, remember! Now let's get some rest and link back up in the morning! Whoop!

I'll see you at the audition, BROntosaurus!

CHAPTER 12

It's Time to Shine, Kid!

This is it. The day of reckoning, crunch time, the showdown, D-Day, the moment of truth, make or break, high stakes . . .

I could go on, but then I'd be late for the audition. Put it this way: It's a very very very very very very very very important day for me (and SFX)! I've spent years at school not saying a word, being a 'nobody' (obvs in their eyes, not mine) and being the butt of Bully Boy's jokes. Now I'm going to show all of them that I am SOMEONE and we are IMPORTANT! Can't lie though, I'm nervous, are you?

Here, on this sliding scale from 1-10 where would you

put the 'OMD I'm nervous!' emoji to show how you are feeling right now?

1 10
_____

I'll come clean: I'm on a solid eleven. Literally losing it! Yep!

Heard of butterflies in your belly? Well I've got dragons! Blood-thirsty beasts with razor-sharp claws and fanged jaws. And these dudes don't flutter, nah fam, they flap their massive, powerful and wild wings AGRESSIVELY. And now my tummy's not just rumbling and grumbling, it's thundering! But . . . weirdly, I'm pleased. It means I want this. The bigger the nerves the better the verse, remember? The worry will bring me words; the concerns, creativity; the anxiety, attitude; and the fear, flavour. Booya! That's what you call flippin' the script! Oh, and REALITY CHECK: I'm actually living my dream, right now. Why? I'm backstage for a rap audition! Can you believe it? Always wanted to be here, and it's even better with SFX, so let's get down to business and start by warming up our vocal chords. All the big rappers and singers in showbiz do this. And here's a few vocal drills I read about online. You can join in too, of course! Let's GO!

1. A Lip Trill

This sounds weird, and you look weird doing it, but just play along for now. Cool?

Make a 'brrr' sound by blowing air through your lips. It should sound like a speedboat. Just imagine you're standing in front of a propeller and then suddenly someone switches it on. What would happen to your lips? See it in your mind? Yep! Now just do that. Easy!

2. The La

This one is really simple. Just say or sing 'la' but hold it for as long as you can. The world record is held by a lady called B-LA-bera which is six hours and forty-two minutes. And that's all they managed to record before everyone got bored and just left her at the top of that mountain doing her thing. WILD!

3. Fanimals

LOL. Yep! I'm laughing before we've even started this one. So is SFX! So, choose two, three, four, five or however many animals you are a fan of. Then, recite the sounds they make in random order as loud as you can. So much fun. Here's some of my favourites:

Cat-Dog = MeoWoof!

Cow-Chicken = MooBawk!

Frog-Dog-Chicken-Horse = RibbitWoofBawkNeigh!

Monkey-Seagull-Lion-Duck = OooOooAhAhCawcaw-RoarQuack!

Bee-Snake-Pig-Owl-Mouse-Sheep = BuzzHissOinkTwit-twooSqueakBaa!

How good does that feel? Proper LOLZ, don't you think?

Feel free to add a few of your own ingenious animal fusions below too. You can use these before you perform. See, I got you!

_____

_____

_____

_____

_____

_____

_____

_____

_____

Brain wave! I was thinking how funny these one-of-a-kind animal hybrid amalgamations would look, and how fun it would be to draw them! It might even be good for my nerves, to help calm them before the big show. Check out my Bee-Dog-Cat-Rat-Frog:

Here's another one. This time you have work out what animals I have used. Answers are at the back of the book!

And guess what? You can now draw your FANIMAL too! Just think of your favourite animals and put them together below. You got this, my G!

I bet your crossbreed combo looks sick!

Right, two more warm-ups and we are ready to roll. Thank the rap gods we're doing this in the changing rooms. Can you imagine what it must sound like from the outside with the random brr, la and animal sounds?! LOL! Speaking of random sounds, number four's a goodun!

4. Jibber-Jabber

To successfully complete a jibber-jabber all you have to do is follow these simple steps:

- Choose one of your favourite songs at the moment
- Replace the lyrics of the song with your own words. But not real words. No! These words must be gibberish, which means made up
- Then you just sing your heart out. But not literally, as you need your heart firmly in your chest to stay alive. And we need you alive, broski!

Here's my rendition performed to the melody of 'Greensleeves' as an example – you know that proper old song that apparently Henry VIII composed . . . hmmmmm:

Hab na skoodoo la goo-doom nyap sa har,

Inding jar raktar

Gib dib dibdib dar,

Caloo coo coo sharoo moo lambroo,

Didim dim zim zim palim shwing zing ding!

Fun, right?

Over to you to create your own warm-up jibber-jabber:

Melody/Song name: _____

Your remix:

_____

_____

_____

_____

_____

Just one more warm-up left, and this one is my favourite!

5. The Ha-Ha

This one pretty much does what is says on the tin: Ha-ha! Yep, all you have to do is laugh, loudly and proudly. But really give it some, my G. You know when you do the whole lean back and let that laugh bubble and bounce from the bottom of your belly all the way up your throat and out into the big wide world. Here are some proper funny ones to try for this warm-up:

- Ha-ha-ha! (The funny one)
- Hoo-ha-ha-ha! (The evil laugh)
- Teeheeheeheehee (The cute one)
- Wahahahahahahahahahahaha (The really evil laugh)
- Hohohohohohohohohoho (The Santa banter)
- Cackle-cackle-cackle (The witch laugh)
- Hee-haw-hee-haw-hee-haw (The donkey/ambulance laugh)

And my final and favourite one:

🔘 The pig!

Here goes: 'Snort snort snort snort sno—'

'Z, what are you doing?'

Whoops! It's Mr G. I swear this guy is an ACTUAL ninja – he's always sneaking up on us.

'The auditions start in ten minutes. Get a move on!'

Ten minutes! Wow! This really is it – the ACTUAL audition is happening! And the queue is pretty short, to be fair. Wait, where is everyone? And where is Bully Boy? Looks like it's just me and SFX, and the Mitchell sisters: Ellie and Khloe. I didn't even know they rapped! But I do smell competition. Hmmmmmm . . . Hold on! Someone's coming out of the audition room now. Sounds like they're crying too. Can't be Bully Boy 'cause he spends his time making others cry. No, it's Valentia and she's proper beside herself. She's the sickest singer in school. Wowza, if she's crying these judges must be brutal!

The dragons in my belly are now fully breathing FIRE! NO WAY am I going into that audition room!

'SFX, do we really wanna do this?' I ask her, feeling proper nervous now.

She looks nervous too. She's pacing and rocking on the balls of her feet. Not a good sign! But suddenly she's giving me that look that people give you when they're about to say something big. Here she goes:

'We've come this far, Z, we can't back out now. We've got this!'

I know she's right, but I just can't do it. I don't care who you are OR where you are in the world, I think you'd probably quit too. So I've decided, yep, it's a big, fat NO WAY from me! I just cant, my G. In fact, to get my point across (especially for those of you all over the world reading this), here are the words NO WAY in multiple languages just so you can get the picture:

Spanish: ¡De ninguna manera!

French: certainement pas!

German: Auf keinen fall!

Italian: Assolutamente no!

Portuguese: De jeito nenhum!

Russian: Ни за что!

Mandarin: 不行 (bù xíng)

Japanese: とんでもない (uso deshou!)

Korean: 절대 안 돼! (Jeoldae andwae!)

Arabic: a! (Mustahil!)

Hindi: बिलकुल नहीं! (Bilkul nahin!)

Dutch: Geen sprake van!

Swedish: Aldrig i livet!

Greek: Με τίποτα! (Me típota!)

Polish: W żadnym wypadku!

'You're not giving up, Z!'

Yep, It's Mr G again! This guy won't quit! Looks like he's
got more to say too.

'SFX is right, Z. Remember, winners never quit and quitters never win!'

Durr, ain't that just really obvious?

Warning: Brain wave incoming! Sorry to go off topic again, but I hate it when people use 'motivational quotes' that just state the obvious. Here are some of my favourites, or should I say worst ones:

1. 'Just breathe'. Uh hum, as opposed to what exactly? Not breathing and droppin' down dead?

2. 'The secret to getting ahead is getting started'. Okay, but what if you are already ahead? This quote is useless at this point, right?

3. 'Every journey begins with a single step'. Well, yeah, otherwise we'd all still be in bed all day every day! Actually, wait! With that being said, every journey therefore actually begins with a single stretch (YAWN!).

4. 'Always give 100%'. What about if you're donating blood? Hmmmmm!

5. 'Success is just around the corner'. Cool, but what if you're walking around in circles?

'This is your time to shine, buddy! And SFX too. Stay positive.'

Told ya. This dude ain't giving up. And I know he's right. I just need a reality check. And look at that! PING! Perfect timing, as I've just spotted a mirror across the room, so now I'm staring directly at my reflection. And do you know what: I suddenly feel kinda good, so I smile. And that makes me feel even better. So much so, I now feel like shouting: You can do this, Neeko, you **RAP GOD**!

WOAH WOAH WOAH! That felt amazing! And did you see what else just happened? I just told you my real name! SURPRISE! The question is: had you already worked it out?

Yes ☐

No ☐

Well done if you did! Either way, my name's Neeko – nice to meet you, my G.

'You can do it, Neeko! You can do it, Neeko! You can do it, Neeko!'

Wow! Now SFX and Mr G are chanting! This is an epic moment, my G! Can you feel the good vibes vibrating through the pages? More than happy for you to get up and do a little celebration shuffle right now if you fancy it?

'WE can do this, SFX!' I say, more determined than ever now.

What a U-turn! I'm now ready to RAP, my G! BUT not in this chapter. Let's do it in the next one! It'll add to the excitement and vibes. Cool? Good! That's settled then.

See you soon, Han S-BRO-lo! (Big up my Star Wars gang.)

CHAPTER 13

We've Got This . . . We Think!

Welcome to the actual, actual audition, my G. Kept you hanging for a while there back in chapter twelve, but I promise that this is now the **REAL THING.** And let me kick this off by telling you something: Eminem was soooooo right in that 'Lose Yourself' song 'cause my palms are sweaty, my knees are weak and my arms are heavy. Yep, I've got all the symptoms of a nervous kidwreck. Here's a little more detail:

a. I'm sweating like a snowman in a sauna

b. My heart is racing faster than a cheetah that's just gulped down a quadruple espresso (that's the really small strong coffee cup thing adults drink)

c. My legs are shaking like a mariachi's maraca

d. My belly is doing bigger flips than an Olympic gymnast!

The worst part is, I have also developed a really bad case of 'excusitis' and it's getting worse by the second. Here's just five of the excuses I've come up with in the last minute to get myself out of here and back home ASAP:

1. I'm not wearing my lucky socks

2. I gotta go 'cause it's my goldfish's birthday party and I'm late. (For the record, I don't actually have a goldfish and if I did it wouldn't even remember who I was or the fact that it was its birthday.)

3. Damn! My shoes are on strike so I can't walk into the room. Too bad!

4. Sorry, I'm allergic to winning so I am going to sit this one out

5. To be honest, I'm too sick (as in good) and too much of a rap legend, so I'll just leave it this time to give someone else a chance

'Oh, snap out of it, Z!'

I look up at Mr G and SFX, but neither of them said that.

'No, it's me: Warrior!'

Wowza! He's back! Where's the GONG, bro?

'No time, Z. Some of us have things to do. Now get in there and DO IT!'

Oh my days! He did not hold back there.

'Nope! I didn't. You need to get a move on, Z! It's time to turn on the turBRO!'

TurBRO! Now I like the sound of that.

'Let's do this, Z!' It's SFX this time, and she means business!

Looks like we're on, my G!! Perfect timing too because Mr G has literally just shoved us in the door.

'Judges, this is Z, and this is SFX. Together they are Beats 'n' Barz.'

Why is Mr G so chilled when my heart is literally doing the Macarena right now? The judges on the other hand are showing no emotions at all. Proper blank slates.

They are all just staring at us. Well, apart from one of them who's pointing towards us. What does he want?!

'Stand on the X, please.'

Looks like it's time to deliver the un-X-pected! You know, the e-X-traordinary! The e-X-clusive, e-X-quisite and the e-X-travagant! Okay, I'm done with the 'X' puns 'cause now I'm standing on the actual 'X'. SFX looks at me. I look at her. And then we do that thing: the synchronized smile, knowing that we're gonna work together and absolutely smash this!

Nothing from the judges yet. They are just writing stuff down, and, you know, being all judgy. One of the dudes looks like Simon Cowell, but a Poundshop version – moodier, shorter and oranger (is that even a word?).

The other dude is wearing a really tight bright-yellow suit. And I mean really really really really tight! So tight if the trousers were to squeeze his legs any more, I think he'd actually POP! Sitting really quietly next to both of them is the one-and-only G-Whizz, last year's Royal Rap Rumble champion. Since winning the battle she has become a global superstar. She's got her own TV show, a triple-platinum album and even her own line of dental floss. It's called Boss Floss. What a legend! Wait. Looks like Discount Simon is about to say something:

'Okay, Z and SFX, Beatz 'n' Barz. When you hear the beep, drop the beat. This is your chance to show us what you've got. Good luck!'

I don't think we need luck, my G. But just in case luck really does work, I've included some famous and well-known 'good luck' charms that might just get us over the line. Feel free to add yours to the collection in the blank box. You never know, they might just work! All you gotta do is touch each one and whisper, 'Good luck, Beats 'n' Barz'.

Four-leaf clover	Lucky rabbit's foot	Horseshoe
Wishbone	Lucky pizza slice	

Showtime! SFX know's our BEAT-cret code. When we hear the beep, she drops the beat. Boom! She is killin' it!

My turn! Oh no. My throat is super dry. It literally feels like I've swallowed the Sahara Desert or just munched on a camel's flip-flop washed down with salt. Not good!

Nothing is coming out of my mouth . . .

'Is his mic working?' one of the judges asks.

MORE NOTHING . . .

I can tell from their faces that the judges ain't impressed. I think they've seen enough. G-Whizz has her head in her hands. You know when your mum or dad says, 'I'm not angry; I'm just disappointed'? Yep, she's got that look going on right now. And then . . .

SLAP!

Now, I've heard of a pat on the back, but that was more like a super-sumo slap on the back. And you'll never guess who just did it! Warrior? Nope! Worrier! Proper savage that!

'SORRY, Z, BUT THERE COMES A TIME IN ALL OUR LIVES WHEN WE JUST HAVE TO TAKE THE PLUNGE. YOU'RE ON A HAMSTER WHEEL TO NOWHERE AT THE MOMENT, SO DO ME A FAVOUR AND DO IT! JUMP IN! FOR YOU, FOR SFX AND FOR THE FUTURE OF RAP!'

Now that's a turn up for this book, innit? Worrier the wrecking ball just smashed some straight-up sense into me. And do you know what: I think it's worked. Let's RAP!

Chorus:
She's the girl who doesn't speak!
That's what they say to me,
But when she beatboxes you'll see,
The music sets her free!

Now drop the beat!
I'm the boy who doesn't speak!

That's what they say to me.

'Cause all my words are locked up in my head,

And I can't find the key!

Verse:

Hi,

My name's Z.

That's the name given to me,

'Cause I've only said

A few words since starting school,

'Cause when I do,

They rhyme,

Which they say ain't cool!

And ever since then they've been cruel.

Nobody says hi to me,

They just walk . . .

On by making up these lies.

Until my eyes can't hold their cries.

It's not nice knowing you're not liked.
It's not right to feel this way inside!
But I find that I feel fine,
And that pain goes away when I start to
write.

Rhyme after rhyme,
Line and line,
And now I'm on this mic telling you about my
life!

A new chapter,
'Cause I am now a rapper,
Here to tell everyone like me:
YOU MATTER!

You're not different,
You're unique!
You not on your own,
You're with me!

And I'm . . .

Chorus:
The boy who's proud to speak!
For everyone like me,
So don't call me Z any more
My name's Neeko!
Yeah that's me!

Mic Drop!

I did it. No way! I. Just. RAPPED! On a microphone. In front
of people. How cool is that? I guess this makes it official:
I'm now a certified rapper. Beatz 'n' Barz are legit. Is it

weird that I want to clap for myself right now? But wait? Why aren't the judges saying anyth—

WOAH WOAH WOAH! If only you could see what I can see right now, my G!

G-Whizz has started that slow clap thing which Mr G has joined in with backstage. One by one, each of the judges have joined in. It's getting faster and louder by the second. And I'm all for it. SFX smiles at me and I flash a grin right back because we know we've done it. Mr G has joined us on stage now too and is giving us the universal rap symbol for 'you smashed it'. BUT WAIT. OMD. What is happening. The judge dude in the way-too-tight yellow suit has whipped his mic from the holder. He is standing up, and raising it up.

It is happening . . .

You know what is coming . . .

Yep, it's the . . .

MIC DROP!!!!!!!!!!!!!

Do you know what that means? The 'RULE OF RAP' automatically comes into effect! See below for an exact extract from *The Book of Rap* detailing precisely what that means:

LET IT BE KNOWN UNTO ALL SUBJECTS, NEAR AND FAR, THAT I, THE RAP GOD, HEREBY DECREE THAT IF ANY JUDGE (EVEN IF THEY ARE WEARING A REALLY TIGHT YELLOW SUIT) AT ANY POINT IN ANY RAP BATTLE 'DROPS THE MIC', THE RAPPERS WHO ARE AUDITIONING ARE (BY DEFAULT) GRANTED EXPRESS PERMISSION TO MOVE ON TO THE NEXT STAGE OF THE COMPETITION.

Did you just read that? Digest that? And even believe that?! We're through! We're going to the Rap Rumble! It's OFFICIAL! Beatz 'n' Barz are ready to conquer the world! But there's so much to do: we need to practise; we need to plan . . . we need an OUTFIT! Yep, you know what that means, my G! It's time to go shopping! Bring on the makeover and then the TAKEOVER! See you in chapter fourteen for my GLOW UP, BROslaw!

Peace!

CHAPTER 14

Let's Shop for Some Bling!

Welcome to the freshest and coolest fashion show in the world, my G! Yep, you can forget the catwalk and all of that prim and proper stuff because this is now the RAPwalk, with serious swagger and sick drip on blast! And guess what? There's only one model who's going to be trying and buying today and that is . . . me, Neeko!

Oh, forget to say SFX is coming too (obvs!) to offer her expert opinion, as is Lil Sis.*

*Sidenote 12: Just do me a favour and ignore my mum in the background. She's only here 'cause she said I can't go shopping on my own. Oh, and she has all of the Ps aka the dough-re-mi aka the cheddar aka the CASH MONEY, my G, and we are going to need that. Lots of it! (Well, some of it. I'm not a global superstar with unlimited dolla dolla bills just yet!)

Check out my rapstar essentials:

Shades	☐
Cap	☐
Ice	☐ → Jewels, not cubes. Duh.
Trousers	☐
Crep	☐
T-shirt	☐
_____	☐

And can you guess the missing tick box item?

_____

Here's a clue, just in case you ain't got it yet. Lots of rappers say _____ is money.

Last chance:

_____

Yep, the answer is 'time'. And how do you tell the time? On a watch! That's the missing item. As soon as you become a rapper, you just have to up your wrist game, my G. You can't rock a plain-Jane watch any more – it needs to bling, standard! And there's so many to choose from: AP, Patek, Richard Millie, etc. But, those are all serious Ps and Mum doesn't look happy right now, so I am gonna keep it nice and easy and just go for a Rolly. You know, a Rolex! All of the rappers have these and for me to be in their league, I've got to get one too. Whoop!

'Time to snap out of it and get in the car, Neeko!'

Wow, she sounds vexed. But the good news is we're

rolling. Next stop: the shops. And can you guess where we're going to cop all of this sick drip? Yep! The big smoke otherwise known as the capital city, London! Booya!

First stop: the big and fancy shops on Oxford Street! I can't wait to walk out of those places with one of those big bags – you know the big yellow one or that shiny green one. People know straight away that if you have one of them in your hand then you have just splurged on a sick spree of retail therapy. And, wow, do I need that. We've been on quite a journey so far in this story, so this is well-deserved for both of us.

Forgot to say, Lil Sis has taken on the role of my stylist for this part of the adventure and I can already hear her saying something about a man bag and spiky studs. Hope I've got that wrong! SFX is pulling samples from the rack. Wow! That's a lot to try on. Better get going and into the dressing room . . . You ready, my G?

The rapwalk is officially beginning! Oh, and if this book does ever get made into a movie one day, this bit is going to be a proper sick montage with the most amazing rap soundtrack, you just know it! So let's do it. Here's outfit number one:

The Old-Skool Rapper

As you can see, I am rocking the classic superstar sneakers with the classic shell-toe design and, of course, those famous three stripes! Then there's the slick zip-up trackie topped off with a bright and bold bucket hat. Boom! Can't forget the signature fat gold rope chain with more carrots than Bugs Bunny's rabbit hole! Too slick, my G. What do you think? Be honest.

Okay, time for drip number two:

The West-Coast Rapper

Now this look is a vibe. Baggy trousers, the matching chequered shirt (top button done up only), crisp white T, bandana and the old-skool Chuck sneakers crep. Too smooth!

But, it still doesn't feel right yet. What do you think? Let's try another look. Here's drip number three:

The East-Coast Rapper

Jeez! This one is fire. Casual, but oh-so-cool and collected. The classic basketball jersey, baggy jeans and those undeniable high tops. So fly! And look at the ice; Frosty the Snowman would be jealous right now. And to round it off, the fitted hat is classic!

What you thinking? For me, this still ain't quite right. Let's try one more. Give it up for drip number four:

The Skater Boy/Girl Rapper

Goodness gracious me. Now this is fire attire! In fact, I got to give this one a clap! The classic skate sneaks with a sick jacket-over-the-hoodie combo, old-skool combat trousers and, of course, the snappiest snapback going. This slaps!

What's your favourite, my G?

Old-skool Rapper ☐

West-Coast Rapper ☐

East-Coast Rapper ☐

Skater Boy/Girl Rapper ☐

I'll be be honest: I like bits from each look, so I'm going do exactly that. I call it the 'Drop Pick' — all of the best bits together to create a new look. Here's the hit list!

A black oversized T

Black baggy combat trousers

White Air Force One style boots

Black snapback and shades

Check it out!

Now that's some serious swagger, if I do say so myself! All we need now is to take a swift trip to Arendelle to link up with my man, Olaf, to get that deep-freeze, iced-out

diamond treatment and we are good to go! And when I say Arendelle, I'm speaking metaphorically of course. It's just an analogy for the jeweller who's going to hook me up with more ice than the North Pole, my G.

'You know you're not allowed to wear any jewellery at school, Neeko.'

Weeeoww weeeoww! Neenaw neenaw! Hold on to your yawns, my G, 'cause it looks like the Boring Brigade is back with their rules and regulations (not Mum, I mean the school!).

'Please, Mum! It will complete my look. How can I be a rapper without any bling? It's impossible! Unheard of, in fact. What am I gonna do?'

'You'll have to work it out I'm afraid as we have to get back to the car before we get a ticket!'

I swear, man, if my mum were to ever form a band they'd easily be called one of the following:

1. The Buzz Busters

2. The Mood Hoovers

3. The Joy Jackers

4. The Fun Sharks

Why can't she ever support my rap dream? That would make me so happy, you know. I'm not asking for much, am I? Okay, okay. I know I am asking for more ice than the North Pole right now, which actually is a lot, but it just seems like she doesn't really care about any of it. She hasn't even listened to any of my rhymes. Proper sob story, I know – but I just wish Mum was a little more interested in my interests. It ain't all about the swag, you know? Anyway, sorry for putting a bit of a downer on the occasion, my G. At least we have a new outfit now; we can work on the bling thing later. Tomorrow is the night of the Royal Rap Rumble final and we have to get some R&R. That stands for rap and rest. Shopping is tiring! You need to rest too, my G. You deserve it.

Speaking of you, you're such a legend – do you know

that? You've come all this way with me and you're still here! And I guess if you've made it this far you really are my BMGFE (Best My G For Ever). A proper BROmance! And to show how highly I rate you – I've got something really cool for you. Check this: It's a graffiti alphabet. Not just any graffiti alphabet – it's the official Rap Pack alphabet! And you know you can't be a rapper or an official part of the crew without your own lit logo. And your one is going to slap! All you have to do is choose a rapper name or just keep your real name, then use the letters below to create a sick logo!

Insert your lit logo here:

Bet it looks epic! ✔ Right, let's get back to business and review that to-do list:

Shades	☑
Cap	☑
Ice	☐
Trousers	☑
Crep	☑
T-shirt	☑

PRACTISE FOR THE COMPETITION! ☐

Aside from our frosty problem, it's been a pretty productive day.*

*Sidenote 13: I was about to check my snazzy new watch there, but I DON'T HAVE ONE! And as bleak and as peak as that is, I ain't got time to wallow.

Meet you in the next chapter, BRO.M.G, for one final rap rehearsal (so we can complete the to-do list) before the big show. Peace out!

CHAPTER 15

Now It's Showtime, Are You In?

Booya! It's time to practise! But first, I forgot to give you this in the last chapter: It's your Official VIP ACCESS ALL AREAS BACKSTAGE PASS to the Royal Rap Rumble Finale!

No WAY!

Yes WAY!

I told SFX you're coming too. She's proper gassed as well. Guess we're now our own little Rap Pack! You know what that calls for? A secret handshake! Follow me:

Step 1:

We AIR SPUD!

Step 2:

Then we SHAKA! (It means 'hang loose' or 'everything will be cool')

Yes, MY G!

Step 3:

This is the final step. Together, we count to three. Like this: one, two, three! And then both say (at the same time) 'My G!'

And that's it! Well, almost. See, there is one more thing you need to know now that you're officially part of the Rap Pack and that's the top-secret, mega-classified Rap Pack password!

Yep, if you ever suspect an intruder or phoney homie in the Rap Pack and they have passed the hush-hush handshake test AND also greeted you with the 'Yes, my G' greeting, then there's only one thing left to do! ASK FOR THE PASSWORD! And to reveal it to you now, you have to have been following every step of the way because the password is the answer to this question:

What is the name of the Rap Rumble judge who won the competition last year?

You got it? Cool! So, our final rehearsal game before the big performance (I've saved the best till last) is 'The Rap Alphabet'.

Here are the rules!

- Choose a subject. Yep, you can rap about anything! (Football, swimming, gaming, school, chess ... whatever!)
- Fill in the alphabet (on the page coming up) with words

that relate specifically to your subject, beginning with that alphabet letter of course

- Once you have written a word, try to find other words that rhyme with it. For example: cat, hat
  Note: The second word doesn't have to begin with that letter; it just has to rhyme!

And listen, you might not be able to complete every letter at first, but please don't give up. Just CHEAT! Yep, you can cheat a little! Here's a sick hack!

Use an off rhyme (that's a rhyme that sorta sounds the same but doesn't actually rhyme perfectly like cat, tap, Caz, dab). This works really well for any rap you want to rhyme! Get it? As long as it sounds cool, is something to do with the subject and sorta rhymes, you're all good, my G!

Oh, a quick tip! Try to choose a subject you are into or want to write about. I'm choosing Nando's, which is the best peri-peri chicken shop near where I live, and as far as I'm concerned it's the GOAT of all restaurants and also my happy place. So, yeah, big up Fernando Duarte and Robert Brozin – the two legends (or should I say geniuses) who invented Nando's and the option to pick how spicy you want your chicken to be. Of course, I go for extra-hot! You?

Here's a small example of my rap alphabet for the letters a–c, all about my happy place:

Subject: Peri-peri chicken

a: amazing   *b:* butterfly chicken   *c:* chilli

And there you have it! The beginnings of an 'Alphabet Rap'. While I go off to finish my alphabet rap (and order some of that sweet peri-peri), you've got time to sort yours too. For now, just add the words that begin with that alphabet letter. Don't worry about the rhymes yet! Off you go:

The Rap Alphabet.

Subject:

a: b:

c: d:

e: f:

g: h:

i: j:

k: l:

m: n:

o: p:

q: r:

s: t:

u: v:

w: x:

y: z:

How did you do, my G? It's not an easy task, I know, but the more you practise this with loads of different (and random) subjects, the better you get at it. Simple! And do you know what else gets better? And bigger?! Your vocabulary bank. Ching ching! And what does every rapper need in a rap battle? Vocabulary! Loads and loads and loads of words. Put it this way, you need to become a Word Wizard, a Vocab Viper and Language Legend if you really wanna be a rap god! So practise, practise, practise!

Oh, and READ! Like Mr G said. It's a FACT! Reading is

the single GREATEST thing you can do to become a sick rapper. Seriously! *They* (here we go again) say you are what you eat; and I say YOU ARE WHAT YOU READ! It's true! Think about it: every word you read and absorb is a new word you can use to write a rhyme or rap. Your words therefore become your ammunition with your mouth, and your microphone becomes your weapon. So load up on those words, my G, ready to fire away on any beat and in any battle.

We clear? Good! But just in case you need me to say it again though: READ, READ and then READ SOME MORE! Picture books, chapter books, graphic novels, poetry, newspapers, comics, magazines, maps, song lyrics, street signs, even the subtitles on the telly with the volume down!

Wicked! I'm glad we've got sorted 'cause now it's time for you to add your rhyming words to your alphabet. Remember: the rhyming word for each letter doesn't have to begin with that letter. Here, check out my example for the letters a–c I did before:

a: amazing   b: butterfly chicken   c: chilli

craving   drippin'   Achilles

Over to you! And when your finished, you can check out

my completed rap alphabet too. Let's Go!

Peri-Peri Chicken Alphabet.

Subject: Peri-peri chicken

a: amazing   b: butterfly chicken

craving   drippin'

c: chilli   d: dip

Achilles   chip

e: extra-hot   f: flame-grilled

guess what?   they filled

g: grilled veg   h: halloumi

peri-peri wedge!   will do me

ledge   foodie

i: iconic
want it!

j: jumbo
gung ho

k: ketchup
step up
best stuff

l: lemon and herb
reckon will work

m: macho peas
nacho cheese

n: Nando's
Nan goes

o: olives
got his

p: Perinaise
any day

q: quarter
water

r: rice
twice

s: spice
nice

t: The Great Imitator
rate ya

u: utensils
essentials

v: veggie burger
further

w: wing roulette   x: extra

get   texture

                        select a

y: yummy bonus sides   z: zesty

boneless thighs   besty

See! There are rules, but there are also no rules at the same time. Just look what I did for 'x' – I used the 'x' sound to start the word not the 'x' letter. Yep – my rap, my rules! Speaking of rap, the next step – once you have your wrapped-up 'rap alphabet' – is to actually write a rap! Whoop whoop! And to do that, just follow these simple steps:

Step 1: Rhyme at the end of each line.

Say it with me:

RHYME AT THE END OF EACH LINE!

Step 2: You can start your rap lines with any letter from your alphabet. It never has to be in alphabetical order, unless you want it to be.

And to help you even more, here's a breakdown of my favourite rhyming patterns you can try, showing you the 'rhyme at the end of each line' rule.

Rap Pattern 1:

Words or a sentence before one of your

alphabet words (alphabet word at the end)

More words or a sentence that end with

the rhyme for that alphabet word.

Here's an example as a rap:

The greatest place in the world is <u>Nando's</u>,

It's so tasty, even my <u>Nan goes</u>.

It's the flavour; it's the <u>texture</u>,

So I can't help but order <u>extra!</u>

See, I have underlined the rhymes at the end of the lines.

Rap Pattern 2:

Words or a sentence before one of your

alphabet words (alphabet word at the end),

Words or a sentence before a different

alphabet word (alphabet word at the end),

Words or a sentence at the end of the line

that rhyme with first line,

Words or a sentence at the end of the

line that rhyme with second line.

Nando's Rap Pattern 2 Example:
I like to order a quick quarter,
With a side of spicy rice. ←
Then wash it down with free water,
And if I'm hungry I'll do that twice! ←

Can you see which words rhyme above? Awesome! Now it's your turn to try it! Then when you're done you can check out my rap. Yep, it's time for . . .

DRUMSTICKS . . . whoops! I mean DRUMROLL, please!

BRRRRRRRRRRRRRRRR!

The Nando's Rap!

The Nando's Rap

Uh oh! I've got a craving,

For a certain food that's amazing!

Yeah, I'm racing straight to a Nando's

It's so tasty, even my Nan goes!

It's iconic!

And I want it!

So I start my order with olives!

And halloumi, that'll do me!

I can't help it: I'm a foodie!

I like flame-grilled,

And when they fill,

My wrap with bare grilled veg.

Big love to the chef, he's a ledge,

For this sweet potato wedge!

Alongside my favourite dip,

And a side of my favourite chips!

But, no ketchup,

'Cause we've stepped up!

To Perinaise: that's the best stuff!

Good texture,

One extra,

That's the starters,

Now I'll select a . . .

Main course! Butterfly chicken . . .

But what sauce do I pick for the dripping?

Guess what?

Extra-hot!

'Cause when it comes to the spice,

I'm a boss!

Or I could do lemon and herb,

Tough choice! What do you reckon

Will work?

Nah, feed me chilli,

Nah, feed me spice,

Why? It's my Achilles,

And I feel nice!

Hey! The Great Imitator,

Is for the vegans, but I still rate ya!

And a side of the macho peas,

Gimme that – why? That's nacho cheese!

I can take it one step further,

'Cause I've heard that the veggie burger,

Is real tangy and real zesty,

Who knows . . . it might be my bestie!

Doubt it . . .

'Cause if I could get,

Anything it'd be the wing roulette!

And a thousand boneless thighs,

With some of them yummy bonus sides!

Or I might just order a quarter?

No fizzy drink, just water!

Or I could go for the jumbo?

Why not? Let's go GUNG HO!

Wait! Did I forget anything essential?

Oh yeah, the utensils!

And that's a wrap (Nando's pun there)! Just imagine if you were to do this every day about a different subject, you'd have a billion words in your vocab bank in no time, and wouldn't have to wing it (another Nando's pun) ever again in a battle. Speaking of battle, I can't believe I'm saying this, but I actually feel ready for the Royal Rap Rumble now! Yep, it's GO time, my G! See you in chapter sixteen, BROnut, for the last dance (rap)!

P.S. Here's a page from my Book of Raps for you to write your own rap using your rap alphabet. You got this!

CHAPTER 16

The Question Is: Will We Win?

Part 1

'Ladies and gentleman, queens and kings, divas and dons, hustlers and homies – it's the moment you've all been waiting for: LET'S GET READY TO RAP RUMMMMMBBBBLLLLEEEE!

Yep! You're live and direct with me, punchline Pete, here at the Flow Factory for the hottest ticket in town and the most anticipated event of the year. Say it loud and say it proud: it's . . . THE BATTLE OF THE BAAAARRRZZZZZZ! And you know exactly what's up for grabs for our rookie rappers to get their gangster grip on, don't you? Uh huh!

You guessed it. THE GOLDEN MIC!!! Speaking of mic, it feels like the right time to introduce our judges for the evening. First up: make some noise for the skin-tight sensation aka Mike Check!'

'Groovy greetings, soul friend. Grateful for the cosmic connection!'

'Well, I have no idea what that means, do you? Thought not! Anyway, while he squeaks into that chair over there, let's meet our second judge and last year's golden mic champion: Go wild for G-Whizz!'

'Hey! Hey! It's time to slay!'

'It certainly is, G-Whizz. It certainly is! And we all know who slays more than Santa on Christmas Day, don't we? He's the kingpin, our top boy and head honcho, the big boss and a BIG BIG deal with BIG DEEP pockets. Everybody give it up for the man, the myth, the legend . . . it's Simon Pow!'

'Hello, everyone. Now let's get on with it – you have two minutes to change your life, just don't waste my time!'

'Straight to the point as always, Simon. And he's right: win this competition and you will change your life for ever! The question is: who will it be? Beatz 'n' Barz or—'

'Z! I'm so glad I found you!'

It's Mr G! I wonder if he's seen SFX? She was meant to be at mine before so we could come here together, but she didn't turn up. I've been looking for her ever since I arrived, but she's nowhere around! I haven't even been able to enjoy this VIP treatment properly without her.

'Hey Z! How are you feeling? Are you ready? Where's SFX? Did you two come together?'

Okay, now I am worried and it's blatantly showing on my face.

'I cant find her, Mr G! And I don't think I can do this without her. No Beatz, no Barz, you know?'

'I tell you what, I'll go and have a look for her. You wait here, and when I'm back I've got something uber cool to give to you. Be right back.'

Uber cool? I've always wondered about that word. One

minute it's an adjective and the next it's a taxi, no? Turns out it's actually German for 'beyond' or 'above'. I guess it's just their version of saying 'sick' or 'lit' or 'hard'. This has got me thinking and do you know what that means? Uh huh, it's time for us to splash into another long-overdue brain wave!

Brain Wave! Yep, to kill some time while we are waiting for Mr G and SFX, why don't we have a look at the word 'sick' in other languages. And when I say sick, I am obviously talking about the cool version, not the vomit. Check these out:

Spanish: *Flipante*

Italian: *Figo*

Dutch: *geweldig*

French: *Trop stylé*

Portuguese: *muito legal*

Japanese: すごい *(Sugoi)*

Do you speak another language, my G? If you do, you know what to do! Write it down below, bruh, so we can build up our own sick 'sick' vocab vault, if that makes sense:

'Sick' in _____ is _____

Anyway, we're getting distracted again – let's move on! I'm seriously worried about SFX now. Where could she be? I hope she is okay! Maybe she was more nervous than I thought? Maybe she's not coming! Nah, she's always so cool and calm – she'll be here, trust me! Anyway, I don't even have any time to wallow; Punchline Pete's about to say something.

'You know the rules, beat freaks. Two minutes each, and what do we want to see? Rhymes, word play, flow, delivery, punchlines, clarity, composure and lots and lots of confidence! No mistakes, oh and . . .

ᴅᴏ NOT CHOKE!!*

*Sidenote 14: Choking in a rap battle is when the rapper forgets their lyrics because of all of the pressure. This causes them to pause as if they have something stuck in their throat. Hence the word, CHOKE! So, yeah, in rap a choke ain't no joke!

'Yep! It's about to go down, rhythm riders – well, someone is! And it's going to hurt BIG TIME: a crushed dream, a soul destroyed and a career in the BIG FAT bin. True story! Why? Well, for the loser of this battle it's going to be worse than slipping on a banana peel in Mario Kart and spinning onto spikes in Sonic! Simply said, they will be a zero and their opponent a hero. Brutal!'

Wowza! Talk about pressure. This is getting proper intense, my G. How are you feeling about all of this? Are you anxious like me? I'm a proper nervous wreck and what's making it worse is SFX ain't here STILL! We don't even know where she is, who she's with AND who we're up against in the rap battle! Oh man, where's Warrior and Worrier when you need them? Actually, why don't we see if they'll come to the rescue now. Great idea! Helllooooooooooo, **WARRIOR** and *WORRIER*, are you there?

'Yes! We are both here!'

Amazing! And perfect timing, guys. So, tell me, what wise words do you have for me today?

'NONE!'

What?

'Yep, you're on your own, Neeko. This is YOUR time to shine! Goodbye!'

Great! Just great! So what now? I wish my mum was here! She'd know exactly what to say right now. Anyway, no point thinking about that, 'cause she's not here, and nor is SFX. This is actually turning into the worst day ever, my G!

'It's time to go back to our top G, Mr Pow, for some words of wisdom. Simon, take it away . . .'

'Thank you, Pete. Just to let you know, my hopes have a flat tyre looking at both contestants' highlight tapes and their road to success so far. AND, on top of that, my expectations just did the limbo – which is surprising because I honestly didn't think they could go that low!'

Savage!

'Well, Mr Pow is certainly fired up today! Let's go to a quick commercial break for a moment so he can have a calm-down cookie and a chill pill. We'll be back soon to meet our rappers, and then it's time to battle! See you soon, flow fans!'

OMD! This is getting proper serious now, my G. I need to get a hold of myself! DEEEEEEEEEEEEEEEEEP BREATH!

PING!

And just like that I feel all right! Why? 'Cause I can see Mr G coming back and he's with SFX! He's also holding two big packages in his hand.

'Found her, and my surprise has arrived too!'

'You okay, SFX?'

'I'm all good, Neeko. Sorry it took me so long to get here. I sorta had to convince my parents to let me compete in the end.'

'Why?'

'Well, at first they thought it was a silly idea. They even said beatboxing isn't a serious career – can you believe it?'

'That's deep! Then what happened?'

'What do you think? I dropped a beat, bro!'

'No way! What did they say?'

'They didn't say anything! They started dancing instead. They absolutely loved it, Neeko. Look! They're over there in the crowd. They can't wait to watch the show now.'

'NO WAY! Now that's epic!'

We both smile and then we do our secret handshake. You know the one I'm talking about, my G. (See, you're part of the Rap Pack now!)

Mr G hands us both a box.

NO WAY! NO WAY, NO WAY, NO WAY! Mr G got us some fresh crep for the show. What a legend! Not just any crep as well, these are the sickest crep I have ever seen: high tops, patent gold and they have light-up soles! Two fire flourishes – remember the rules?! These are going to look epic on stage!

'Now, Z, before you open this next one, have you got a pair of warm gloves to wear?'

Gloves? Inside? In the middle of summer? What? Why would I need gloves?

'Because it's about to get ICY COLD!'

One second: did he just say ice? As in ice ice? As in bling? As in OH MY DAYS please please please say he did and this is about to get real North Pole in here.

OH

MY

GOODY

GOODY

GOSH!

He did! Mr G has got me a chain! My very own diamond-
dripped, iced-out, gemmed-up rapper chain! And the
best bit: there's a microphone hanging from it that has
more diamonds than an engagement ring factory! This
thing blings! Put it this way, an emperor penguin would
need to wear a blanket and a pair of Uggs around me!
True story, Dory!*

*Sidenote 15: Again, not saying your name is
Dory or anything — just rhymes. Like 'Ruth' and
'truth', remember? Also, I know this probably ain't
real diamonds or anything, but I don't really care.
It looks sick around my neck, so I am rolling with it.

He hands a matching chain to SFX too. We are proper

kitted out now!

'Thanks, Mr G!' we both say at the same time. Then Mr G turns to me with a big smile on his face and says, 'Suits you, kid. Or should I say, Rap Kid!'

Rap Kid! I like that! In fact, let me say it again: Rap Kid! Wait a sec, did we just discover my official rapper name? What do you think, my G?

I like it! ☐   That slaps! ☐   Heck to the yeah! ☐

Now that's legendary! This is starting to feel really really real, my G. What an adventure! What a moment!

WAIT! What in the actual rap universe is HE doing here?

'Guess who's back!'

Yep, I'll give you one BIG fat guess who's back, my G. Oh, and don't forget to put your answer on a postcard, please (see below):

Your BIG FAT GUESS:

No Mercy Street,
Tough Town,
Sneer City,
Crusher County,
H8 T3R

Yep, you guessed it: Bully Boy! He's back! BIGGER and BADDER than ever! But why? What is he doing here? It doesn't make sense! Unless he knows the other rapper I'm battling. Yeah, maybe it's just that? Could be? Well, anyway, we're about to find out 'cause it says we're live in . . .

5

4

3

2

1

'And we're back like a boomerang, folks! Who's ready to get this show on the road? Make some noiiissseeeeee!'

Wowza! This is loud, my G. Seriously loud! This is going to be a battle to remember!

'And what a match up we have for you today! So let's get into it, my people. First up, in the red corner, this dynamic duo are fresh onto the scene like a pair of new kicks – crispy clean and full of big dreams. They're coming straight out of primary school still smelling like school dinners and old plimsoles. Give it up for the one the only, Beatz 'n' Bars aka SFX and Rap Kid!!!'

This is like a movie, my G. They're cheering SO loudly as we walk onto the stage. It's unreal. They love us and we haven't even done anything yet! Even SFX is excited!

'And now it's time to introduce their opponent, ready to turn those big dreams into a nasty nightmare. He's the king of the intimidation; the heavyweight of humiliation; a rhyme-wrecking, mic-checking, spine-bending invasion! Yep! He's BIG! He's BAD! And tonight he looks really really MAD! From the depths of Whoknowswhere, it's the microphone mischief-maker, the soul-snatching, butt-scratching rap terminator! Make some noise for Satan's sunshine, it's ... **BULLY BOY!**'

Pause for a sec! Did he just say Bully Boy? Let me rewind that again, just to double-check ...

'BULLY BOY!'

Okay, one more time. This time in slow mo:

BULLY BOY!

Yep! I can confirm that he just said Bully Boy, and I can also confirm that this adventure is now OFFICIALLY OVER!

Now you know why there's a part two in the chapter — to give me moment (or a zillion) to process this. And with that being said, I'll see you on the otherside, my G!*

*Sidenote 16: Of the page that is — for part two, I mean.

P.S. We're doomed . . . BRO!

Part 2

Okay, I've tried every trick in the book, my G. I've pinched myself, punched myself and even slapped myself! Anyone would think it's the first of the month. Anyway, none of it has worked! Meaning, this is definitely not a dream! **IT ACTUALLY IS A NIGHTMARE!** Out of all the rappers in the world, the one I'm up against is my biggest enemy and arch-rival, AND it's happening now. Like NOW, now!

'You can do this, Rap Kid,' says SFX. 'We both can. He might be a bully but he's still just a boy. We got this!'

I smile at SFX.

'You've got this, Beatz 'n' Barz . . . Well, I hope you do, 'cause it, or should I say someone, is about to go down. But before they do, or don't and become our champ, we have to hear them rap. It is a Royal Rap Rumble after all! And with that being said, can we all make some noise and raise the roof for Beatz 'n' Barz!'

The crowd go wild, then quiet. This. Is. It. No more stalling – it's time to shine! Perfect timing too because

I've just spotted a sign. No, not a sign as in an epiphany or spooky signal. No! A literal sign, and guess who's holding it? Here take a look:

It's Mum! She made it, and I'm made up! She is gonna hear me rap! And do you know what? She's right! Mums are ALWAYS right, remember! And thanks to her, I now know exactly how this battle is going to go down. Yep, it's time to be kind! Check this, my G!

'SFX, drop the beat!'

Hey Bully Boy,
It's great to see you,
Welcome back!
Can I kick this battle off by
saying I really like your hat!
And that t-shirt you're wearing adds
to your swag,
What a perfect match!
Man, you deserve a clap!
And I really like the way you've
always got so much to say,
And how you walk around with
all that anger on your face!
It's so impressive how
you get so aggressive,
And never let anyone stand in your way!
Literally,
You kick them,
Punch them and hit them,
Even if they're little, delicate and innocent!
Nothing's stopping you!
You are so magnificent . . .
A master of destruction,
disaster and belittling.
But what's so significant,
Is the reason for your ignorance.

And after all these years of abuse,
I think I've figured it,
Out . . . you're insecure, bro,
A little boy who's hurt,
And you put others down to raise
your own sense of worth.
Low self-esteem has made you really mean,
You bully to look powerful but
inside you're really weak!
It's not your fault though,
Attention's all you seek,
'Cause you probably were neglected growing
up as a little G.
And now you play the tough guy to cope
with all of your trauma,
When you just need a positive role
model to call on.
You need a remedy,
A double dose of empathy,
And to let go of the jealousy,
'Cause I am not your enemy.
You need trust,
You need love,
Do you know what, bro?
You need a hug!

MIC DROP!

'No way! Rap Kid is hugging Bully Boy. And . . . Bully Boy is hugging him back! What a moment! What a battle! And wait! What is happening now?! I think Bully Boy is crying. He is! Sobbing, in fact! The crowd can't believe it! I can't believe it!' Can you believe it?'

Yes ☐   No ☐

'Well well well, we did not expect that! And by the looks of it, nor did Bully Boy! And look! There's more! I think Bully Boy is going to pick up the microphone. He is! But what can he possibly say now? Over to you, Bully Boy, over to you!'*

*Sidenote 17: This is where we cue that tense heartbeat sound effect that you see in all the movies, my G. You know, the one that goes BADUM BADUM BADUM to build tension and excitement?! And here it goes . . .

Badum badum badum . . .

'I'M . . .

I'M . . .

I'M . . .

S . . .

SO . . .

SORRY!'

'NO WAY! He said it. He said the S word! That's it! It's all over! The battle is done. The battle has been won. Not just in rap but also in the classroom, the corridors and the school playground! Some serious lessons have been learned today, and I am proud to say Beatz 'n' Barz are your winners! Yes, SFX and Rap Kid are the new Royal Rap Rumble champions!'

We did it, my G! We won! We're officially rap gods! This deserves a massive WOWZA! And you're going to shout it with me. You ready?

3

2

1

WOWZA!

And now it's time to bleat too! Why? Well, why do you think? Ah, come on! You know who bleats, don't you? GOATS! And that's us! Me, SFX and YOU, my G! Legends, titans, giants, icons and heroes! Speaking of heroes, here come Mr G and Mum.

'You did it, gang! I'm so impressed! You do know this is the start of something special, right?'

'I agree, Neeko, my not-so-little boy.' It's Mum! And she looks so . . . so . . . so . . . (I can't believe I'm saying this) HAPPY! 'This is your purpose, your passion and your amazing talent, son. You have shown all of us here that kindness is never wasted and it always makes the difference. Your little sister and I are so proud of you, darling. And, dare I say it, we would love to be part of your Rap Pack too! Can we join?' Mum grabs me and pulls me into a giant grizzly bear hug. SFX's family have joined us too and are now doing the same to her. Everyone's squeezing till we're wheezing. Now that's love!

'Rap Kid! SFX! Please give us a few words for the camera and everyone back at school watching right now.'

The announcer's here now with the film crew and he's shoving a giant camera in our faces. But what am I meant to say, my G? You know I'm no good at these things. But wait! SFX is pointing at her jacket. Maybe she wants to let

Pete know something? Huh! Wait a second! She's got her finger on a part of her jacket that has nothing written on it. No way! Does this mean that she's . . . it does! I think she is actually going to speak in public . . . Go on, SFX!

'Thank you! Thank you for this chance to speak up. Not just for myself, but for all of the kids out there who feel like they can't. Because being shy or lost for words in this world doesn't mean we are weak or that we don't have big ideas and even bigger dreams. It just means we might need a little more time, a little more space and a little more understanding, that's all. So please be patient with us, and above all: please be kind. If you do, great things will always happen!'

'Wow! We have ourselves a standing ovation! SFX and Rap Kid are not only the Royal Rap Rumble winners but they are also the people's champions – even Simon Pow is crying! This is unbelievable!'

It really is, my G. It really is! Mission complete. And, what an adventure it has been! We are officially the greatest of all time! The GOAT!

I turn to SFX and start to say 'WE ARE THE GOA–'

'Uh hum!'

Uh oh! Guess who's back?!

Phew! It's only Mr G.

'Sorry, Rap Kid. But technically you're the greatest right here, right now, but not of all time.'

What does that even mean? Why is he trying to dampen our dreams. Not cool, Mr G. Explain yourself.

'Throughout history there has always been a GOAT: the Ancient Egyptians, the Ancient Greeks, the Romans, the Vikings, the Tudors, the Victorians . . . you name it, they all had their GOAT rapper. So, technically, for you two to be the actual GOAT, you need to battle and win against all of those other rappers first.'

'And how am I going to do that? Travel back in time? That's impossible!'

'We'll see about that. Actually, do me a favour and just hold that thought – I'll be back!'

'Wait, where are you going now, Mr G?'

'To see a man about a time machine! I'll be back soon.'

Time machine? NO WAY! Are you thinking what I'm thinking is going to happen next, my G?

Your official prediction:

_____

_____

Yep, I think we're on the same page. So now what? I mean, usually at this point in a chapter I'd say something like, 'See you in the next chapter, BROski'. But with this being the end of this adventure and book, we can't do that. Hmmmm, so what next?

Time for a brain wave! And this one's a goodun.

Fancy joining me on another Rap Kid mission? This time going back in time to battle every rap legend that's ever

existed throughout history on the most exciting epic rap adventure ever?

Yes   ☑

Oh yeah! I took the liberty of filling this one in for you, my G. Why? 'Cause we're in this together, remember?! Rap Pack for LIFE!

And with that being said, there's only one other thing left to say . . .

See you in book two, Little BRO Peep!

Booya!

Rap Dictionary/Glossary Thingamajig

Air spud: A non-contact fist bump

Bait: obvious

Barz: lyrics/raps

Big Man Ting: grown thing

Bling: jewellery/diamonds

Booya: an expression of joy

Bougie: posh/fancy

Buss: do

Bussin: amazing or wearing

Butters: ugly

Calm: all good/cool

Crep: trainers

CR7: Cristiano Ronaldo

Dankest: coolest/most epic

Dead: terrible

Drip: stylish clothes/attire

Endz: area/place

Fam: family/crew

Gassed: very excited

Homie: friend/mate

Ice: diamonds

Lit: amazing/cool/epic

No Cap: no lie/for real

Nuda: nothing

Peak: negative/not a good situation

Peng: nice

Poker Face: straight face

Ps: money

Salty: hostile/angry

Sick: wicked/cool/nice

Slaps: excellent/amazing

Slaying: performing at a high standard

SNM: say no more

Spit: rap/speak

A Touch: result or a fist bump

Wasteman: loser

Wowza: OMD/No way/an expression of excitement

Yard: house

Rap name Generator:

Welcome to The Rap Name Generator, my G!

The rules are simple:

1. First, go to box one and find the letter that your first name begins with. Then, just write down the word that's next to it. Easy!

2. Go to box two now and find the letter that your surname begins with. Guess what happens next? Yep! You then write down the word that's next to that too!

3. The best bit: put them together and BOOM! That's your rapper name!

Good luck, BROski!

BOX ONE	BOX TWO
A ASAP	**A** Assasin
B Big	**B** Blaze
C Cool	**C** Cash
D Dolla	**D** Diamond
E Eazy	**E** Enigma
F Fly	**F** Fresh
G Ghost	**G** Ghetto
H Hood	**H** Hustle
I Ice	**I** Impact
J Juicy	**J** Jinx
K Kid	**K** King/Kool
L Lil	**L** Legend
M Mr/Miss/Missy	**M** Monster
N Nitro	**N** Ninja
O Ol'	**O** Outlaw
P Prince/Princess	**P** Prophet
Q Queen/Quantum	**Q** Quest
R Raw	**R** Rebel
S Slick	**S** Savage
T Tricky	**T** Turbo
U Ultra	**U** Unique
V Vibez	**V** Vandal
W Wild	**W** Warrior
X Xplosive	**X** Xclusive
Y Yung	**Y** Yout
Z Zen	**Z** Zilla

Answers

Sneeze Jokes:

1. A shoe!

2. Cashew!

Sneeze Riddle:
A blackboard

Fanimals:
Cow-Chicken

Rap Pack Password:
G-Whizz

Acknowledgements

Wowza! From writing hooks to writing books! Can you believe it, my G?! It certainly has been an adventure, and just like Rap Kid's there are some serious VIPs who have bopped beside me on this rap road to success. Yep! This crew deserves all of the mentions, flowers, love and big respect, because without them none of this would be possible. FACTS! From the get-go they have believed in me, my mission and the fluorescent future we all have ahead of us: a wicked (as in good) world where books and reading remains the coolest thing on the planet (aka the G.O.A.T!). So, without any further delay here's my 'MY Gs' List:

The Grammar Gang:
Big up Uncle Chris (who's not just an uncle; he's also a mentor, my manager, a best buddy, my right-hand man and an absolute LEGEND! You believed, Mr Pluto, and we achieved. No limits now!), Liz (you are a Wiz and a Wonder), Ashley (you are The Visionary and The Guru), Jenna (hands down The Social Media Sensation), Jimmy/ Dimitri (aka the famous and oh-so-fresh DJ Replay), and King Leonidas (aka Leon aka The Camera King aka The True Believer aka The Volcano Predictor aka The Day-1 Don. What a journey, bro!).

The Simon & Schuster Crew:

Yas (my epic and awesome editor: always there, even during bedtime story time – now that's love!); Rachel (thank you for believing in me and taking a chance on my buddy, Z); Laura (your energy is always a vibe, and I can't wait to hear you RAP!); Millie (my sidekick editor and overall superstar – big love!); Dani (You. Have. Smashed. It. With. The. Sales! Say Whaaaat!); Alan (you have brought my vision to life, my man! Thank you); Jesse (thank you for just getting 'it' and of course then getting it done better than anyone on Earth. True G!); Jess (never stressing and always impressing! Thank you for getting the campaign going and flowing); Ali (thank you for your wisdom and sick – as in epic – skills!); Alesha and Dan (the marketing masterplan has only come together because of you two, and I can't wait to make it all happen now and go and meet Rap Kids from all around the world!).

Not forgetting Sorrel, David, Kate, Teän, Alice, Sophie, Maud and all of the export, sales, rights, design, marketing, publicity, production, inventory, digital and audio crews. Big up your amazing selves!

To the Mitchell Massive:

Mum (I still remember the magic and wonder you conjured with every bedtime book or classic tale you told me as a little boy: I am a reader and now an author because of you and all that you have done and still do. I love you x); Dad (you are the G.O.A.T. of storytelling. Hands down! Oh, and the motivation master. Thank you for introducing me to all of those books of power. I have learnt a lot from them and you!); Sharon (no matter what, you were always there . . . and you still are. Thank you x); Chris, Maria, Cousin Noah and Roman the Showman (thank you for always believing in me and cheering me on. I always feel your love wherever I go!) Pierce (you'll always be P Nut to me and my lickle bro – keep shining!)

The Nicholaous:

I also want to shout out my Dada, Nikos. Your kindness never goes unnoticed. You made my experience at university a positive place of learning and always happy times. I am forever grateful for your support x

Can't forget the real OGs: my bapou, Yiacoumi, and angel yiayia, Angela. I am going to keep making you proud and representing the Nicholaou name, I promise. Σαγαπώ πολύ x

The Andronicous:

Helen and Nicos. Thank you for all of your unconditional love and support. I immediately felt like part of your family even from our very first meal together (remember those massive salmon slices aka The Chicken of the Sea?) and still do to this very day! Big hugs to both of you x

Andrea:

Thank you for being my 'hype woman' in every stage and on every stage of this wild ride. From the UK to the US and wherever next! I don't care where we go or how far we fly, just as long as I have you by my side. I love you x

Ellie, Khloe, Tia and Neeko:

From the second you were all born, many of my favourite magical moments together have been snuggled up with a good book. Now I have written my own story, I can't wait to get cosy and read Rap Kid in the same way. But it gets better this time: you're all in the story! Now that deserves a WOWZA! And YOU all deserve the world. Just know that everything I do is for you. For the now, as a family together, and for your future. Believe. Achieve. Succeed, my Gs! Daddy loves you more than Arsenal, Thai Sweet Chilli Sensations, movie nights with salty popcorn, Wagamama ramens and Nando's chicken! Lion, Penguin – I love you! X

Final few thank-yous:

Love and hugs to the old-skool Church Hill Primary School crew in Barnet (especially Rebecca The Dreamweaver and Ray the Diamond Geezer), my teaching journey started in those corridors and classrooms. Big up to the Livingstone family (special shout to Mr Madle, Stu and Mr T) for giving MC G a platform to read and rap. And one final and EPIC THANK YOU goes to you: the reader, aka my G! Keep reading and keep rapping!

MC Grammar 😎